I0684400

An Indestructible Mountie

Adventures of the First Woman Mountie. Book 3

LAURIE SCHRAMM

Print ISBN: 978-1-9994940-4-9
ePub ISBN: 978-1-9994940-5-6

Laurie Schramm

12 September, 1942

My Dearest Willie,

Burn this letter as soon as you have read it.

By the time you get this I will either have succeeded in my mission, or died in the attempt.

Do not sorrow for me as, either way, I will have done my part to ensure the success of the Fatherland in this war.

We will soon be landing in a remote part of North America to install a secret weather station that will guide our U-boats to success, but there is another, hidden mission. A secret within a secret. If all goes well I will

DEDICATION

To Kent,
who served as a CELE Officer in the Royal Canadian Air Force.

CONTENTS

ACKNOWLEDGMENTS

Many thanks to my supportive readers, C/Supt. William Schramm (Ret.) who also kindly allowed my main character to borrow his Regimental Number, Ann Marie, Katherine, Moira, Jayme, Karen, and Ernie for their comments and suggestions on drafts of this book.

LIST OF CHARACTERS
(IN ORDER OF APPEARANCE)

- Max Lichte, graduate student (atmospheric physics), Heidelberg University
- Corporal Leonard (Lenny) Dwyer, radio technician, 14 Wing, Canadian Forces
- Sharon Sanders, graduate student (biochemistry), Dalhousie University
- Dr. David Keen, physicist, DREA, Canadian Forces
- Constable Alexandra (Alex) Houston, RCMP
- Assistant Commissioner George MacLeod, RCMP Security Service
- Silver, an Alaskan Malamute; and Alex's friend and companion
- Staff Sergeant Robert (Bob) G. Simpson, RCMP Security Service
- Dr. Parke, Chemistry Professor, Dalhousie University
- Sergeant Ian (Scotty) Scott, Quartermaster, RCMP HQ Division
- Dr. Alan Grey, Chemistry Professor, Carleton University
- Captain Donald (Don) Harrison, Military Intelligence, Canadian Forces
- Marcus Light, Co-Owner, Oceanside Antiques, Ingonish
- Anna Miller, Manager, Ingonish Beach restaurant/bakery
- Henry Miller, Chef and Baker, Ingonish Beach restaurant/bakery
- Wilma Light, Co-Owner, Oceanside Antiques, Ingonish
- Constable Jack McDonald, former recruit colleague, RCMP.

Laurie Schramm

Cst. Alexandra Houston

1 FIRST PRELUDE: 1942

October 25, 1942

Max Lichte (the Englishers always pronounced it, incorrectly, as 'Lite')
was standing on the bridge, looking out at the rocky cliffs that could just barely
be seen through the thick fog and low-hanging clouds. Everything looked cold,
and grey, and barren. "What brought people to such a forbidding place?" he
wondered. As a teenager, he had visited North American cities like New York
and Montreal and had arrived by steamship in a civilized fashion. This was
something completely different.

The first thing he'd noticed had been the fog and clouds, which blanketed
the churning sea down below. The second thing was the rock. Now and then a
bit of fog, or cloud, or both, cleared providing a glimpse of a wall of rock rising
vertically up from the crashing waves on the shore. He knew from his briefing
that there was a bit of beach there – somewhere - and a way to climb up the
rocky cliff, but at the moment he could see neither, making the cliff appear
forbidding and unassailable.

The third and fourth things he noticed simultaneously. One was the cold. It
wasn't just the cold, or the wind, it was the dampness in the cold and the wind.
Dampness that seemed to penetrate through his parka and uniform clothes. The
other thing was the pitching and rolling. Although it was a great relief and
privilege to be granted a few minutes on the bridge, breathing in the fresh air,
the damp cold exacted a heavy price.

Unlike the relative luxury of his previous trips on ocean liners to this
continent, this trip, which had been on a U-boat, had been miserable. U-687
was one of the newest submarines. Referred to as Type VIIC/41, it was based

1

on the "workhorse" design that characterized most of the U-boats in the fleet but had a few significant improvements over earlier models, particularly its active sonar and stronger pressure hull, giving it a deeper crush depth of well over 300 metres. This latter feature was important for a U-boat that was to be used for secret missions and, to help maintain security, U-687 had been listed on the official register as never having been deployed[1].

Although it was the most modern submarine in the fleet, it was not built for comfort. They had left their base at Kiel in September of 1942, in high spirits, with everyone looking forward to the adventure, and to their chance to prove themselves against the Allies. Inside the pressure hull, the submarine's effective size was only 50 metres in length by less than 5 metres in width[2] — not a lot of space to share on a long-duration voyage with fifty-one officers and crew. After a week of life in the confinement of U-687, the adventure had been stripped of its glamour, and the journey had simply become a burden to be endured. By four such weeks, it had become unbearable.

Max had been plucked out of university, Ruprecht-Karls-Universität Heidelberg (Heidelberg University), where he had been studying atmospheric physics. He had been attracted to the idea of becoming a scientist and learning to do scientific research, but it had been the development of applications of science that had interested him the most. Of the many applications of physics, it was the world of atmospheric physics and the relatively new field of radio-wave transmission that interested him the most. The former had become his scientific specialty, and the latter his hobby. In fact, he had just finished building his latest, and best, short-wave radio transmitting and receiving set when he'd been called into Herr Professor's office to meet with two strangers. The strangers were obviously military men, despite their civilian clothes.

Herr Professor had a name, of course, but everyone in the university simply referred to him as "Herr Professor," and there was an uncharitable rumour going around that his wife referred to him as Herr Professor as well.

Herr Professor had originally built his reputation in meteorology, the physics of weather, and in recent years had shifted his focus to the development of weather-monitoring instruments. For some reason, this had brought him to the attention of the military, and Max knew that a secret project had been underway in a locked laboratory in the attic of their Physics Building. It appeared that Max was finally going to be brought into Herr Professor's confidence.

"You know my interest in weather and weather-monitoring stations?" This was a rhetorical question, of course. "Then you should also know that we have been working on ways to make automatic weather stations — stations that can monitor the weather and transmit the weather information by radio signal, all *without the need for human hands!" Herr Professor had then sat back, complacently as if awaiting applause.*

Max had tried not to disappoint him and launched a volley of questions about how it could be done, how to automate the data gathering, how to assemble it for transmission, and of course, how the radio transmission would be done and what transmission distance would be needed. Max's focus on the technical aspects had clearly pleased Herr Professor as they provided him with an opportunity to deliver a lengthy lecture on such aspects. It did not, at first, occur to Max to wonder why someone would actually want an automatic weather station.

The strangers answered this last question first. The military wanted automatic weather stations so that they could be placed in strategic locations around the world and used to deliver precise weather information for the air force and navy. Especially the navy. The military men explained that weather information was particularly difficult to obtain in remote locations that might be of interest for future invasion landings, ship movements, and ... U-boats hunting convoys.

In the North-Atlantic Ocean, weather forecasts were important for both sides, as they had a profound influence on the planning of naval convoys and the U-boats that hunted them. For the Allies, bad weather meant opportunities to conceal convoys and hinder enemy aircraft. For the Germans, bad weather meant good hunting. Weather forecasting was straightforward for the Allies, who had a large network of ground-based weather stations that could take advantage of the general trend for weather fronts to move from west to east. In contrast, the Germans had to do what they could with specially equipped aircraft and ships, which was both inefficient and dangerous. A better option might be for Germany to have their own weather stations on the North American East Coast.

At the military's urging, Herr Professor had secretly developed a new kind of weather station, one that was quite small, self-contained in terms of power and processes, and automatic in function. If successful, such stations could be secretly set-up wherever they might be needed, from which point they could send coded weather information to offshore U-boats for as long as the batteries lasted, or until the batteries were replaced. Other than the battery replacement issue, the stations should not need human intervention once they'd been landed and set-up. It was at this point in the narrative that all three men looked straight at Max.

"What has all this to do with me?" Max had asked.

One of the military men said that Herr Professor had done the Fatherland a great service by developing the automatic weather station, which had been successfully tested, not only in our attic laboratory but also near one of our own naval bases on the coast. Now it was time to send one out into real service. What it had to do with Max, they explained, was that it would have to be shipped in pieces by U-boat, taken ashore at the right spot, re-assembled in place, and set into operation. For this, they needed a specialist, someone who could not only deliver and set-up the station but who could, if necessary, make any last-minute adjustments or repairs that might prove to be necessary. "With all respect to Herr Professor," they explained, "this is a job for a younger man." They all had looked at Max again.

Max had agreed to do it, of course. It was his duty to the Fatherland, it sounded interesting, and it sounded like an adventure.

It had felt like an adventure too when they'd assembled the two large, inflatable rubber rafts on the forward deck of the U-boat, but an adventure of the terrifying kind. The Captain, an Oberleutnant zur See (Naval Lieutenant), was under orders to find a desolate place on Canada's East Coast, to conceal the weather station. Accordingly, the U-boat had anchored near Cape Breton Island, offshore the south end of Broad Cove, near Red Head. This was well north of Ingonish, the nearest town, and well away from the closest inhabitants.

The weather had not improved, the cold was damp and bitter at the same time, and the submarine was pitching and swaying. The two inflatable rubber boats were not very large, but they took up about half of the forward deck, with the boat crews and equipment taking up the rest. One had to move carefully to avoid being swept overboard!

Eventually, they had launched the two boats and their crews had paddled them to shore. Once there, everyone pitched in and helped to carry the components across the narrow beach, and all the way up about a hundred feet to the top of the rocky cliff. They carried everything on their backs, the ten cannisters, the masts, the instruments, and the stakes, wires, and cables. Fortunately, they had enough people to do it in one trip as each boat carried eight sailors, one with an officer, and the other with Max and a Coxswain.

In the forest fringe at the top of the cliff, Max assembled Wetter-Funkgerät Land (Weather Radio for Land) number one, or WFL-1. The primary cannister contained the measuring instruments, a telemetry system, and a radio transmitter. There was also a ten-metre-high antenna mast and a shorter mast that held an anemometer and a wind vane. By placing WFL-1 well back from the cliff's edge, at the edge of the forest fringe, it was hoped that it would avoid detection. The rest of WFL-1 comprised nine more cannisters, each of which was about 1.5 metres tall and about a half metre in diameter, and each of which housed sets of heavy nickel-cadmium batteries to power the station.

They'd waited for evening to surface and anchor the submarine, so by the time Max was able to begin assembly, it was in near darkness. When it was done, Max set the station to broadcast weather readings every six hours, using a two-minute transmission at 3940 kHz and made sure that it was operating. The station was designed to operate for six months using three-hour intervals, but Max had reduced the frequency of transmissions in order to have enough power for the "secret within a secret" package in battery canister number nine. This was the special secret that he should not have referred to in his letter to his girlfriend Wilhelmina (Willie).

With their cargo disembarked, the submarine left for home. They had spent less than twelve hours near the Canadian coast and had carried out their mission undetected. They didn't have much opportunity to celebrate, however - U-687 never made it home. It was sunk by an RAF bomber in late November, near the Norwegian coast.

Canadian Forces CP-107 Argus

2 SECOND PRELUDE: AN ODD COINCIDENCE

March 16, 1977 – 34 years and 4.5 months later.

The Canadian Forces (CF) CP-107 Argus reduced altitude for another pass along Cape Breton's eastern shore. The Argus was on a mission: to seek out and identify a British submarine that was acting the role of the hunted in a NATO[3] hide and seek exercise. The submarine's mission was to approach Canada's East Coast by stealth and fire a dummy torpedo at an old Second-World-War observation point near the mouth of the Halifax Harbour.

Designed specifically for marine reconnaissance, the CF Argus was widely regarded as the best anti-submarine warfare (ASW) aircraft in the world. Its mission, along with five other Argus aircraft that were spaced-out along Nova Scotia's eastern coast, was to find and identify the sub before it could get into position to attack. If they were successful in locating the sub, then the exercise would shift to that of capture or destroy. If U.S. or Canadian surface ships from the exercise happened to be in the target area, then the mission would be turned over to them. If not, then the Argus was well equipped to handle the job itself. It was only carrying dummy weapons today, but in a potential combat situation, its forward and aft bomb bays could carry eight thousand pounds of torpedoes, bombs, mines and depth charges.

Although the Argus was capable of carrying a flight crew of

fifteen, today it held fourteen: three pilots, three navigators, two flight engineers, and six radio technicians (radio techs). Four of the crew were resting or sleeping in bunks near the galley. The remaining ten crewmembers were at their posts, intent on their mission.

In the belly of the Argus, Corporal Leonard (Lenny) Dwyer was hunched over his console trying to concentrate on his readings over the constant, roaring drone of the aircraft's four large turbo-compound engines. The noise, long hours, uncomfortable seat, and sickly greens and blues of his meter readouts and CRT[4] monitor screens made concentrating difficult. They had already been airborne for nearly ten hours since taking off from Canadian Forces Base (CFB) Greenwood, which was in southwest Nova Scotia – diagonally all the way across the province from where they were now.

Their flight plan called for a twenty-hour reconnaissance[5], so Lenny's shift was about to end, and he was looking forward to being relieved, so he could take a nap in one of the bunks. Scanning his instruments for what seemed like the millionth time, everything looked normal: search radar, signals from the sono-buoys they'd dropped, the magnetic anomaly detector (MAD), and the relay from the shore-based SOSUS station[6]. He was just about to request an explosives-drop, to try another go at explosive echo ranging (EER) when he heard a soft buzz and a light flashed on the instrument panel to his right.

"What's up?" asked his replacement, who had come forward to be ready for their shift change.

"Not sure," replied Lenny, "the new BS detector just went off."

This was properly called BSRFDET (Broad Spectrum Radio Frequency Detector), and it was an experimental radio scanner they'd been carrying for the past week. It was the brainchild of DREA[7] and was designed to scan a broad spectrum of radio frequencies in hopes of detecting any submerged submarine that was incautious enough to be sending a message ashore or to another vessel. Like everything military, the machine had an acronym, and like many things military, there was a slang term for it. Inevitably, BSRFDET was known as the "BS Detector," and there was talk of installing one in the mess hall.

Lenny's complete attention was now focused on BSRFDET and, having thrown the switch to relay the sounds it had detected to his headphones, he manually fine-tuned the frequency detector.

"That's odd," he muttered. "There's a signal coming in on shortwave at 3940 kHz. It's not voice, it's not Morse, and ... [continuing to listen] ... it sounds like a telex signal."

"A target, you think?" his replacement asked.

"No, it's in the wrong frequency range, it's the wrong signal type, and ... there, it's gone."

"Did you grab it?"

"Got it!" Lenny said, looking up above the instrument panel where a reel-to-reel tape recorder had automatically begun recording as soon as the warning light and buzzer had been triggered.

Lenny continued to listen, but the signal did not reappear.

"Well, time for me to relieve you," said Lenny's replacement. "I'll keep an eye on the BS Detector and let you know if it comes back."

"OK, thanks," said Lenny, as he levered himself out of his station's jump-seat and ambled aft for a snack in the galley. As his replacement was donning his headset, Lenny called back to him, "Keep the tape, will you?"

Later, lying in his bunk, Lenny was having trouble getting to sleep. Usually, the drone of the engines and the vibration of the aircraft, coupled with the fatigue from concentrating on his instruments for a full shift helped him to fall asleep, but he was still thinking about the strange radio signal. "It doesn't make any sense," he thought. "It sounded like a telex signal, but it wasn't on any of the usual telex frequencies for weather data or communications."

Lenny eventually fell into a light sleep as the Argus, having found nothing actionable, rumbled off to search another map quadrant.

The next day, and still thinking about the mysterious radio signal, Lenny decided to make a copy of his notes and the tape recording and, together with a brief explanatory note, sent them off to the Electromagnetic and Acoustics Laboratory at DREA – Dartmouth. This made him feel a bit better about it all, but he was sure that nothing would ever come of it.

Lenny was wrong.

Red Head, Cape Breton, Nova Scotia

April 16, 1977.

Sharon Sanders was not, at first, having a great day. Her research project in biochemistry at Dalhousie University had stalled, again, and it was beginning to feel like she would never be able to complete her master's degree. As a result, her stress level had risen to the point where she was having trouble sleeping.

Thinking that a complete break might help, she'd taken a day off and driven north from Halifax for a trip to scenic Cape Breton Island. Following a surprisingly relaxing five-hour drive, she'd stopped at the famous Keltic Lodge resort and treated herself to lunch. Although great for lunch, the lodge was too expensive for her, so she checked in at a small bed-and-breakfast in nearby Ingonish Beach. Then, with time for a brief hike, she debated where she should go and pulled a topographic map of the area from her backpack.

Having been to this area several times before, she'd already done the well-travelled trails just north of the nearby town of Ingonish, one to Middle Head, and the other to Lakies Head. The map showed another point of land, however, that might be interesting. Halfway between Middle Head and Lakies Head was something called Red Head. There might not be much of a trail, but according to the map, it was only about a 1 mile from the highway. It shouldn't be too difficult to reach, she reasoned, and it should offer good views of the ocean and of the coastline in both directions.

Deciding to give Red Head a try, Sharon drove the short distance up the highway, parked off to the side, grabbed her backpack and headed east towards what the topo map suggested would be a cliff rising about a hundred feet above sea level.

At first, it was much more difficult than she'd imagined. The trees were surrounded by thick, shoulder-height brush, and she had to pull, elbow, and push her way forward. Every twenty or thirty feet she had to stop and catch her breath, which may have been just as well since it prompted her to check her compass each time. This, in turn, directed her to make slight course changes at almost every stop, so they at least served to keep her from going in circles, she thought to herself.

After the sixth such stop, it seemed like she'd been struggling through the forest forever, and it felt like she must soon be in danger of reaching the cliff face if she wasn't careful. Pausing to reflect though, convinced her that six stops must only add up to something like 120 to 180 feet – meaning that she had something like five thousand feet still to go. That was discouraging!

"Maybe this wasn't a good idea after all," she thought.

Sharon wasn't the type to give up easily, however, and she decided to try a few more segments of bush-whacking and then re-evaluate.

The next four such segments were no different from the last, and although she was pretty sure she knew exactly where she was, she was rapidly becoming convinced that this particular stretch of forest, was basically impenetrable.

"Maybe just a little more," she thought.

Pressing on, nothing seemed to be changing, and she was finally ready to admit defeat and turn back when the brush cleared, just a little, and she found herself standing on what looked like a game trail. It was narrow and moderately overgrown, but it was definitely a trail and it appeared to head more or less east, toward the cliff. Thinking that this seemed promising, she followed the trail.

Now Sharon was able to increase her pace and decrease the frequency with which she checked her compass. Stopping about every two hundred feet, her compass indicated that the path meandered a bit, but she judged that it deviated about equally to the northeast, then the southeast, then back again, and so on so that she was pretty sure that the trail was still taking her where she wanted to go.

Eventually, Sharon's persistence was rewarded with the slow brightening of her surroundings that meant that the tree density was thinning out and allowing more sunlight to penetrate the forest. Accordingly, she slowed her pace a bit and was glad she did as the forest finally came to an abrupt halt about twenty feet from the edge of the cliff.

Finally!

Approaching as close to the edge of the cliff as she dared, she judged that she was about a hundred feet up from the ocean, and roughly at the broad summit of this particular stretch of cliff. Her orienteering skills had clearly served her well, as she was almost exactly at the position she'd intended to reach.

With a happy sigh, Sharon sat down near the edge, took her pack off and pulled out her water bottle and a plastic bag of GORP[8] for a well-deserved snack while she enjoyed the fantastic views of the ocean below, and coastlines to the north and south. Munching away, and consulting her topo map again, she relished the thought that not many people would have fought their way to this particular spot. Other than the trek though the dense forest, a person could probably hike up along the ocean-facing ridge from the north or the south, where in both cases the cliff eventually and gradually sloped downwards towards the ocean. Either of those would be a long, and possibly treacherous hike though. On balance, she decided, the route she'd taken was probably the easiest of the three.

Fortified by her snack, and having reveled in the unspoiled location, fresh ocean breeze, and scenic views, Sharon decided that she should start back as she still had to preserve some energy and alertness for the long drive back to Halifax.

Shrugging her daypack onto her shoulders as she was about to re-enter the forest, she momentarily lost her balance just enough to cause her to step to one side of the game trail. This was also just enough for her hiking boot to catch on something unseen in the long grass, and just enough to cause her to fall to that same side.

"What the hell was that?" Sharon thought as she picked herself up. She wasn't hurt but she was annoyed at herself for tripping, and fully prepared to take it out on whatever her boot had gotten caught on. Crouching back down, she pushed the long grass, first one way and then another, until a glint of dull metal appeared. Continuing to push the grass around she discovered a rusty length of stranded wire rope attached to a ring, which in turn ran through a hole at the top of a metal stake that just barely protruded above the ground.

"Someone must have pitched a tent up here," was Sharon's first thought. "But who in their right mind would carry wire ropes up here just to tie down a tent?" was her second thought.

Her natural curiosity aroused, Sharon instinctively pulled on the other end of the wire rope, expecting to see a frayed end snake its way toward her out of the grass. Except that instead of coming free, the wire rope immediately pulled tight and lifted out of the grass, at about a 45 degree-angle. Getting up, she followed the rope. It seemed to go a short length to just inside the edge of the forest.

Sharon just stood there, staring, with her mouth open.

***

Laurie Schramm

May 2, 1977,
Defence Research Establishment Atlantic (DREA),
Dartmouth, Nova Scotia

It was a cloudy, foggy, and rainy Monday morning, ... again.

As Dr. David (Dave) Keen jogged from the parking lot to the rather ordinary-looking brown-brick building in which his Electromagnetic and Acoustics Laboratory (EAL) was housed. Entering through the main doors, he gave his raincoat a shake to dislodge the worst of the water it was carrying and headed for the stairs. Despite its official name, EAL comprised not just a laboratory, but three laboratories, several offices, and a high-head engineering area, in the latter of which were assembled instruments and prototypes before deployment on ships or submarines for field testing and demonstration.

Reaching his office, he shed his raincoat, dropped his briefcase on a side chair, and headed for his main lab, which served as the nerve centre for his little research group because it housed the coffee machine. With coffee in-hand and having said "good morning" to his lab technologists, he returned to his office and immersed himself in a continuation of his previous week's intensive study of the latest results from their experimental anti-sonar technology. Pausing only occasionally to make a circuit of the bathroom and then the main lab for more coffee ("You didn't buy coffee – You only borrowed it" he always thought), Dave remained single-mindedly focused on trying to make sense of the latest data until he heard a distinct "plop" sound, at 11:30. The plop sound announced the arrival of the morning's incoming mail in his wire 'In' basket.

Happy now, to have an excuse for a mental break, Dave got up to check out the fresh mail. On the top of the pile of inter-office mail envelopes and fresh technical journals was a large, brown envelope. Picking up the envelope, his eyes went to the return address on the label:

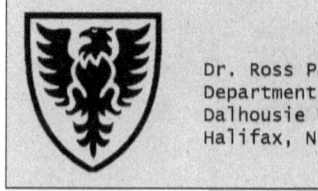

Dr. Ross Parke, Killam Chair,
Department of Chemistry,
Dalhousie University,
Halifax, N.S.   B3H 4R2

Ross was a friend and former fellow Dal[9] graduate student from days gone by. Suppressing the urge to revisit old memories from his grad school era, Dave opened and then shook the envelope, and picked up the note and photograph that fell out.

The photo showed what looked like a radio mast surrounded by dense forest and bushes. Nearby were what looked like miniature oil drums poking their heads up above the tall grass. Old ones if he was any judge, as they seemed to be covered in rust.

The note from Ross said that one of his graduate students had encountered this strange looking apparatus, surrounded by trees and bushes, but close to the edge of a high cliff overlooking the ocean. She had taken a picture of it and shown it to Ross who, knowing Dave's interest in things related to radio waves, had thought to pass it on to him.

Dave really did have some interest in radio waves and had done research on acoustics for his Ph.D. in Physics, but he mostly maintained an illusion of continuing interest in conventional radio to provide cover for the nature of his real military research on torpedo detection and evasion systems, which had more to do with sonar than radio. As a result of this slight misdirection on his part, Dave received a fair number of leads on things he wasn't really interested in, like this one ... except that, in this case, the location seemed to ring a bell.

"Cape Breton," Dave thought, "and on the east coast, ... hmmm."

Walking to the back of another of his labs, Dave went to a bank of filing cabinets, one of which was labelled "Dead Files." This was where he kept the odd things Dave's various colleagues occasionally sent him. Unless they truly interested him, he generally kept such files for a year and then, if nothing else related to them arose, they were either destroyed or sent elsewhere for deep storage, just in case. The package from Maritime Patrol Squadron was easily found as it was the most recent of the odd referrals. Pulling out the file, his eyes again went to the return address label:

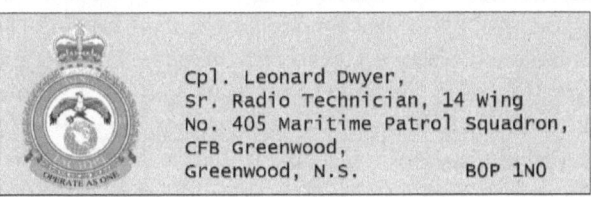

Cpl. Leonard Dwyer,
Sr. Radio Technician, 14 Wing
No. 405 Maritime Patrol Squadron,
CFB Greenwood,
Greenwood, N.S.   B0P 1N0

15

"Lenny," he thought, as he re-opened the package. Shaking the package, a reel of magnetic tape, some photocopies, and a hand-written note fell out. He'd looked at all this when he'd received it the previous month. It was unusual, but not rare, for operational techs to send him recordings of strange signals. Usually, they were odd radio or sonar signals, and they generally ended up being classified as instrument malfunctions, or noise, or simply "unidentified." In any of those cases, the incident would be logged and forgotten. Re-reading the note and the copy of the signals log from Lenny, Dave was inclined to think that this one would fall into the latter category, but he thought he may as well re-play the tape anyway.

Walking over to one of his other labs, he spooled the tape onto one of the compatible taper recorder/players and put a set of headphones on to listen. It definitely sounded like Lenny's description: something made by a machine, definitely not Morse, something more like telex.

"A short burst of telex on an odd frequency," Dave muttered to himself. "Nothing to do with the sub-hunting exercise Lenny had been on," he'd decided when he first listened to it in March and listening to it again didn't change that opinion. It certainly had nothing to do with his own sonar work, of course. Contrary to what a lot of people thought, or assumed, sonar and radio had little in common with each other beyond the fact that waves were involved.

According to Lenny's log, it had been a very weak signal too. Dave's original conclusion had been that it was probably some kind of private-sector transmission, and most likely a ham radio operator[10] playing around. He'd scribbled a note to that effect and put it all away in the Dead Files cabinet. The log also contained the aircraft's coordinates at the time they'd picked-up the strange signal.

Walking back to another of his labs Dave pulled open a chart drawer and, flipping through the contents, removed the Canadian Hydrographic Service nautical chart that covered northeastern Cape Breton, #4363 "Cape Smoky to St. Paul Island." Taking it over to a large table, Dave spread out the chart and identified Red Head, near Ingonish, just like Ross had said in his note. Dave placed the end of a ballpoint pen over the location of Red Head.

Now, picking up the note and log Lenny had sent, he ran the

forefinger of each hand along the approximate latitude and longitude noted in Lenny's log.

More interested now, Dave grabbed a ruler and fine-tuned his identification of the location at which Lenny and the Argus had received the strange radio signal. Placing the end of a mechanical pencil at this point he stood up and looked again at the chart with its two makeshift markers.

"I'll be damned …"

3 CALL TO ACTION

"Will you do it?"

"Arrgh! This again."

My name is Alexandra Houston. My friends call me Alex.

In the summer of 1974, I'd been 24 years old, and feeling like my career was at a standstill. I'd studied chemistry at university and liked it, but not enough to pursue science as a career. I'd reset my sights on police work next and joined the Metropolitan Toronto Police force (Metro). Although policing seemed like a better fit for me than science, my two years with Metro had mostly comprised routine administrative- and traffic duties. These assignments were important, and needed to be done by somebody, and done well. But for me, they didn't fit the Hollywood vision of policing that I had developed, and I hadn't found them to be very challenging.

They say you should be careful what you wish for.

My life soon changed drastically, beginning with an unexpected meeting. Without explanation, my Captain had sent me to go and see a Royal Canadian Mounted Police (RCMP) officer that wanted to meet me. My reaction to this was apprehension, and I wondered what I could possibly have messed-up so badly that it had caught the notice of our national police force.

That's how I first came to meet Assistant Commissioner George MacLeod. After a lengthy conversation that I belatedly realized was an interview, he told me that he had asked my Captain (his friend) to recommend one of his young officers for a special pilot project he had in mind. He wanted someone who wanted to accomplish things, someone eager and tenacious, *someone chomping at the bit to be allowed to do some 'real' police work, and ... someone female. At this point he had shed his stern 'Mountie look,' relaxed his entire body, chuckled, and said that my Captain had recommended the "biggest pain in the butt" in his Division -* **me**.

Assistant Commissioner MacLeod had explained that the 'Force' had fallen behind the times and that its senior leadership wanted to build a more diverse police force. "We're going to be recruiting immigrants, visible minorities, maybe even people with some kinds of disabilities as well," he said, "But we have to start somewhere, and that somewhere is by engaging women." He wanted to try a first "pilot test" with a woman, but that pilot test had to succeed as it would pave the way for an entire first troop of policewomen that would follow. He had thought of using someone that had already qualified as a policewoman, and simply re-train them in the "RCMP way."

That had brought me up to full attention. "Wait a minute! Do basic training all over again?"

"Yes!" he'd replied, "that's the only way you can possibly succeed. In the old days of the Northwest Mounted Police, a person could get appointed straight into the Force, even as a commissioned officer, if they had the right political connections. No more. Now everyone starts out the same way, as a Constable, and by going through the same basic training. If you want to have any hope of being accepted, much less respected, that's how you have to begin."

So, that's what I'd done. I went through training at the RCMP's Depot Division training centre in Regina, dealt with the good and the bad issues that came with being the first woman to train there, and survived to become the first woman Mountie. I hadn't intended for it to happen, really. The opportunity just came and found me.

After training, or re-training if you like, I'd been posted to Radium City, a small town in very northern Saskatchewan that, in its early days, had been a great uranium mining centre. Although my new boss, Corporal Morrison, had told me that nothing interesting ever happened around there, he'd been wrong, and I'd had to rescue him from a mine collapse, run our entire detachment single-handed while he was confined to hospital for six weeks, get rescued by a strange dog from near-death, solve a mystery, and find and catch a murderer – all in only four months!

The dog was named Silver. Investigating a mysterious series of break-ins had led me to some unusual places, including several abandoned uranium mines. In one such mine, I'd fallen through a trap and found myself hanging precariously over the sharp edge of a raise, a kind of vertical mine shaft. Unable to get out and tiring fast, I was saved by the almost magical appearance of what I first took to be a wolf, which gave me quite a scare, but turned out to be

Silver, an Alaskan Malamute. Silver somehow sensed that I was in danger, had decided to help, and with his assistance I had been able to climb up and out of the raise. To make a long story short[11], while I'd continued to investigate the case, he had attached himself to me, was eventually given to me, and we'd been close friends ever since.

Sometime later I'd found myself in another surprise meeting with the same Assistant Commissioner MacLeod. Once again, a 'coffee meeting' had turned into an interview and, once again, he had something new in mind for me. By this time, he'd become head of the Force's Security Service[12] and, unsurprisingly, he had some ideas he wanted to try out by way of some experimental pilot projects.

"Like me?" I'd asked.

"Exactly," he'd replied. It turned out that he now wanted me to go and work for him in the Security Service. Of course, he could have just ordered me to go, but he wanted me to go willingly, and immerse myself in his new plans.

And then, just like he'd said over a year previously in Toronto, "Will you do it?" and just like at our previous meeting, I'd said, "Yes, Sir."

That had taken me to Ottawa in November of 1975. I'd met my new supervisor in the Security Service, Staff Sergeant Robert ("Call me Bob") G. Simpson, and been introduced to the shady worlds of spies, counter-espionage, anarchists, and terrorists.

"Surely, we don't have any of those in Canada?" I'd asked.

"We did, and we do," Bob had answered and had illuminated me with a number of fascinating, yet somewhat discouraging 'intelligence' stories.

"Like you, most of us thought we were safe here in Canada" Bob had begun. It went downhill from there, from the Second World War, through to the Cold War. Despite Bob's chilling stories, my first Security Service assignment hadn't been counter-espionage but a domestic threat. A series of bomb threats directed at two oil sands companies in northern Alberta had led to Silver and I being sent undercover to investigate.

Our path to the oil sands was indirect, however, as Silver and I were first sent to Innisfail, Alberta, to be trained as a police dog and handler team. "If that dog is going to go everywhere with you, then we should get him trained too," Assistant Commissioner MacLeod had announced, on one of his periodic visits to see how my orientation was coming along. Both Bob and Assistant Commissioner MacLeod had been interested in the possibilities presented by the first female Mountie, especially undercover possibilities, and they were also interested in, and seemingly amused by, the notion of me having Silver along as a kind of side-kick.

After training in Innisfail, Silver had officially joined the Mounties too and we were sent up to Fort McMurray, undercover. We'd made an interesting pair. At that time, I was the first and only woman Mountie, while Silver was the first and only Alaskan Malamute police dog in the RCMP. The notion that no one would suspect us as being undercover police succeeded pretty well and had at least held up for long enough for us to identify and apprehend the bomber, although not before a few more adventures. In one of those adventures, I'd been able to save Silver's life, which evened up the score and reinforced the feeling I'd long had that our destinies were inter-twined.

***

May 10, 1977,
Security Service offices,
RCMP "HQ" Division, Ottawa, Ontario

"Hi, Bob. What's up?"

Staff Sergeant Robert G. Simpson, my boss, had summoned me to his office.

"Morning Alex," he replied. "I want to show you something. Have a look at these." He motioned with his hand to several objects that were spread out across the front of his desk: some hand-written notes, some photocopies, a photograph, and a reel of magnetic tape.

I read the notes first, then glanced at the photocopies, and looked more carefully at the photograph. Knowing there would be more to come, I looked up at him and raised an eyebrow inquisitively.

"There are a few people scattered here and there around the country that know that I'm in the Security Service and that I have an interest in odd coincidences," he said.

I nodded knowingly.

"These arrived Friday from a colleague in defence research, who's based in Dartmouth," Bob explained. "People send him odd things too. These arrived at his labs within a few weeks of each other. He didn't see any reason for the military to be interested but noted the geographical connection and sent them to me."

"OK," I said. "Do we have any reason to be interested?"

"Well, we have one or two additional pieces of information," Bob said, leaning back in his chair. "Have a look at this," he said, pulling another photograph out of his desk drawer.

What he'd handed over was an 8 x 10" black and white, glossy photograph of a bunch of cannisters that looked a bit like miniature oil drums, arranged in some kind of obscure pattern and connected by what looked like a bunch of guy-wires. Near the centre of the pattern were two masts, one taller than the other.

"What's this?" I asked.

"First take another look with this," said Bob, handing me a large magnifying glass.

Scanning the picture with the magnifying glass, I could now see that the guy-wires were supporting the two masts, the taller of which had some kind of box attached to it partway up its length, and the shorter of which had two little devices mounted at the top.

"Is that an arrow on top?" I said, and then before Bob could say anything, "no wait, it looks more like a wind vane."

"A wind vane and an anemometer," agreed Bob. You are looking at a picture of a small automatic weather station."

"It looks old," I commented, voicing my first thought.

"Very old, in fact," confirmed Bob. "It's a Second World War era German *Wetter-Funkgerät Land*, or WFL, automatic weather station. During the war, the Germans set up a few of them here and there in the North Atlantic to provide weather information for their ships and submarines. This one was discovered earlier this year on the east coast of Labrador[13]. Now compare the two photographs."

Reaching for the smaller photograph, I could see in a glance that they were pictures of the same thing. "You can't see very much of this one with all the trees and bushes in the way," I commented, "but now that I know what to look for, they look the same. Did it get moved?"

"No, I think this is another one."

"Are we interested in old German weather stations?" I asked.

"Not by themselves, no. But I wonder whether this one has been put back into use."

"The batteries would have died long ago, and if it's been reactivated, it wouldn't be for weather information," I muttered, still looking at the photographs.

"I agree," said Bob, "but there's something intriguing about a hidden radio transmitter sending low power transmissions in code, don't you think?"

"In code!" I exclaimed, sitting up straight.

Bob grinned his Cheshire Cat grin that I knew so well. He loved to let these little secrets of his out, bit by bit. I didn't mind. I sensed that it was his way of coaching my thinking processes.

"In code," he said firmly. "Our signals people are working on the transmission that the Argus picked up. All they've been able to determine so far it that it's in some kind of code – they don't even know what language has been coded, although English or German are high on their list of possibilities."

"Any idea what's going on then?" I asked.

"One or two. Give me your thoughts first," said Bob, still in coaching mode.

"OK," I said, thinking about it. "Suppose someone has access to an old war-time weather station and transmitter. They don't need the weather part because they can just listen to any radio station for that."

Bob nodded.

"They could use the transmitter to send messages if they replace the batteries and feed their own signal in – is that hard to do?" I asked.

"I'm told that these old stations took the signals from the weather instruments and fed them to some kind of converter that turned them into telex messages and sent them out. Our people think that you could type new messages on a teleprinter machine and have them come out as a series of dots punched onto a strip of paper. They say that you could then take the paper strip, plus a handheld paper reader, and read the data into the relay circuit of the weather station, and have the station send the signal out. Apparently, it would only require a bit of rewiring in the relay circuit."

"OK, so it can be done," I said. "The next question is why go to all this trouble just to send telex messages by radio? Presumably to avoid detection…"

"That's what I think," said Bob. "According to the military, the signal they received was weak. If it came from this old station, then we have someone sending coded messages, at low power, from a hidden location, and I'd like to know why."

"Yes," I agreed. "Of course, it could be legitimate. Some kind of hobbyist or history buff maybe, or some kind of industrial secrets?"

"What do you think?" Bob asked, with the Cheshire Cat grin back on his face.

"No, I don't really think so either," I admitted.

"You're right that whatever it is could be perfectly legal," Bob, changed tack. "Or the signal and the weather station may not be connected at all, but I want to be sure." Bob paused, and then said, "There's another reason... do you remember the reading you did last year on the construction delays at the Cape Breton heavy water plants?"

I did remember. Canada's nuclear reactor development program was focused on natural uranium fuel, moderated by heavy water[14]. The reactor designs were called CANDU (CANadian

Deuterium Uranium system). In order to build CANDU reactors, our nuclear industry needed uranium (which was mined in Saskatchewan and refined in Ontario), and heavy water. The heavy water came from two large plants in Cape Breton, one in Glace Bay and one in Port Hawkesbury.

The reasons these sites were chosen were partly technical (availability of suitable water and power) and partly political (economic development). The second reason had unintended consequences, because these plants created a lot of jobs for construction workers from the two small towns and their nearby communities, at a time in the late 1960s when their economies were really struggling. They not only provided jobs but relatively high paying jobs, especially when overtime was required, which happened more and more frequently as the projects fell behind schedule. The Port Hawkesbury plant started-up in 1970, not far behind schedule, but the Glace Bay plant continued to suffer set-backs. Ultimately, a series of suspicious construction and equipment failures had caused so much alarm that Atomic Energy of Canada Ltd. (AECL) and the Province of Nova Scotia had both asked the RCMP to investigate the possibility of sabotage. Naturally enough, the RCMP was concerned that this could be a new chapter of Cold War activity.

It turned out that there *had* been acts of sabotage, and the RCMP had discovered that the Glace Bay sabotage was caused by some of the workers themselves, who wanted to keep the construction project alive for as long as they possibly could, to keep their jobs alive. The overtime pay issue hadn't been thought of in advance, but once it had become obvious that there was money for this, it just provided an extra inducement to continue to sabotage things. Ultimately, the RCMP had discovered the people behind the sabotage and foiled their plans but hadn't found enough evidence to be able to press charges. The files on the people concerned were kept 'open,' but otherwise, the saboteurs lost their jobs but avoided prosecution. With construction progress restored the Glace Bay plant was finally completed and had only just commenced production the previous year (that is, in 1976, some eight years behind schedule!).

"I thought that the conclusion was that the sabotage was due to workers wanting to continue working, and not from foreign agents?" I asked, shaking myself back in to the present.

"That's the official conclusion, yes." Bob agreed. "But I've always wondered whether there was foreign influence behind the scenes. We know, from other sources, that the Soviets are interested in the heavy water technologies – both the CANDU reactor technology and the heavy water production technology. We suspected that there may have been a plot, not only to delay our construction program but to use the delay to try to steal our know-how."

Bob sighed. "There were indications of a shadowy presence behind the scenes but nothing definitive, and we eventually had to let it go, but I've always wondered if there was an agent in-place somewhere."

"Or is still in place?" I asked.

"Could be," Bob replied. "I'd like to send someone in, under cover, to snoop around and find out … will you do it?"

There was the perennial question. "Sure," I replied.

"Not so fast," Bob cautioned. "We've just strung together a whole series of 'what ifs,' so you might discover that it's all just our overactive imaginations, or something innocent, or at least something legal…, but if it's really some kind of espionage game then it could get dangerous."

"Dangerous how?" I asked.

"If we have an agent in place, it could be a civilian that's been suborned, or it could be someone better trained. Either way, if your cover gets blown and you scare them enough or corner them, they may strike at you without warning, and strike to kill. So, if you go in you'll be going alone. If you get into a situation and don't have the time or resources to call in for help, then you'll have to look after yourself. I have confidence in you, but I want you going in with your eyes wide open."

"I can bring Silver?" I asked.

"I wouldn't have it any other way," Bob laughed.

Bob's concern had gotten me thinking about personal security, so before leaving Ottawa, I paid a visit to the "HQ" Division's Quartermaster and explained in very general terms what I was going to be up to.

"So, what do you want from me?" Sergeant Ian Scott growled. He was clearly another of the Force's ubiquitous crusty Sergeants.

I explained that I'd been issued a snub-nosed Smith & Wesson '.38 Special' revolver when I'd gone undercover in Alberta and that it had been reasonably easy to conceal in the clothing I'd worn in northern Alberta's cold Fall through Spring seasons, but now I'd be working in the summer and was interested in something smaller.

"Huh," he'd said. "Did you ever shoot the snub nose?"

I had, and I related the tale of my close brush with a bomber armed with a rifle against my little revolver, but with which I'd managed to bring him down after he'd shot Silver and was about to do so again."

"So, you know from experience how inaccurate a snub nose is," he growled, "and now you want something even smaller?" My brush with death had softened his attitude a little, but not by very much.

"I do," I replied firmly. "I need something I can carry securely, and conceal, even if I'm only wearing a T-shirt and shorts."

"You don't ask for much!" he growled again, but I could tell he was thinking about it as he looked me up and down as if examining every contour of my body.

Being examined so closely made me feel uncomfortable, but I held my ground, glared at him, and tried not to blush.

Seeing my reaction, he relented further. "Call me Scotty," he said with a sigh, "and don't worry, I'm not leering, I'm thinking …"

Finally, he shook his head, and said, "I think this is crazy, but you're the one that has to survive in the field, not me."

"Come along," he said with a wave, motioning me to follow him to the back of the armory. There, he opened a cabinet and rummaged around a bit before giving a satisfied grunt and pulling out a small cloth bag, which he handed over to me."

Opening the bag, I discovered a fancy looking silver derringer with pink hand grips. As I looked back up at Scotty, he smiled for the first time, saying "We confiscated that from an American fraudster who was plying his trade out in Alberta. He used to wear cowboy boots, and he had the habit of carrying the derringer in his boot. Sounds like a tale out of the Wild West of the last century, doesn't it?"

"He obviously got caught," I observed.

"Caught yes, but the fraud charges didn't stick, and he was acquitted." There was a pause, and he grinned, "But he was convicted of carrying, and concealing, a restricted weapon – the one you're holding now. We usually collect up this kind of confiscated junk and send it out in batches to be melted down for scrap, but I like to keep the odd thing around just in case."

"Does it actually work?" I asked, looking at it dubiously.

Scotty chuckled, "Now you're starting to sound like me," he said. "Yes, it works. What you're holding there is a Remington Derringer. This model is called the 'Mama Bear,' and it was designed specifically for women. The idea is to be easily concealed in a purse or stocking[15].

As I continued to examine the little gun, Scotty showed me how the two barrels pivoted upwards for reloading, and how a cam on the hammer alternated, when fired, between the top and bottom barrels.

"It looks like a toy," Scotty continued, "especially with the fancy silver plating and the pink pearl hand grips but looks are deceiving. It has a trigger guard, which is unusual in a derringer, but I like that for safety. It's about as small as you can get, with only a 2.5" barrel, and this particular model takes .38 Special rounds, the same as your snub-nose and your regular-issue revolvers, so you only need to carry one kind of ammunition. It's only effective at close range, but at close range it can easily kill."

"Thanks, Scotty," I said gratefully, "I'll figure out some way of carrying it."

"Tape it!" he said.

"What?"

"Tape it. Forget holsters and purses. If you want to conceal it get some first aid tape, pick a likely spot on an arm or leg, and tape it there. You'll always be able to carry it and find it easily, no matter how many... or how few, clothes you're wearing. If you get into a tight spot and get searched, chances are it will be overlooked as a bandaged injury. If you need to draw it, just tear away the tape."

Ouch, I thought.

Scotty smiled, correctly reading my mind. "Lesser of the evils..."

"OK," I said, "I'd never think to look for something like that on a suspect, so maybe no one else will either."

I hesitated.

"Yes?" Scotty, asked, with an air of extended patience.

"Since you obviously have an eye for this kind of thing, I was wondering about a knife."

"A knife?"

"Well, kind of a survival knife, but small, and concealable, and something that could also be used for self-defence in a pinch."

"You don't ask for much do you?" The gruff tone was back, but I could see that he was thinking, so I just waited silently.

After a moment, he went back to another cabinet at the back of the armory and rummaged around for a while before appearing with another cloth bag, which he was about to hand-over when he thought better of it and opened it himself. "I'd better show you this one first," he said.

Opening the bag, he withdrew what looked like a very small, black, rectangular box made of metal. It was only about five inches long and very narrow and thin.

"Watch," he said, as he pressed a tiny button that I hadn't noticed at first. As soon as he did, there was a "click," and a blade hissed straight out from one end.

I jumped involuntarily.

Grinning, he said, "This is a small, modified version of a military UDT knife[16]."

"Like a switch-blade," I observed.

"Something like that," he agreed, "except that with a switch-blade the blade swings down and around on a pivot. They were popular with street gangs in the 1960s because the swinging blade alone could be an intimidating sight. This one is more functional than fancy. As you can see, it's automatic – you push the release and the blade springs out from the front-end. The blade is stainless steel and partially serrated, so it will cut through almost anything. The blade is only two and a half inches long, but you can still cut with it... or kill with it," he added grimly. "The handle is made from aircraft-grade aluminum so its light but strong. The whole thing only weighs one ounce."

"You said it had been modified," I prompted.

"Yes, in fact, the only reason I kept it is that I've never seen one like this before. Look here," he said, turning the knife around. "Someone made an entirely new handle for this. It's very much like the factory original, except that it's a bit longer so that right behind the spring mechanism there's just enough room for this."

With a flourish, he twisted and pulled on the handle's end cap, which popped-out to reveal a piece of dull grey metal protruding from the inside of the cap.

"Magnesium!" I said.

"Ferrocerium," Scotty corrected. "Same idea though. Ferrocerium is a metal alloy you can strike with a knife blade to create extremely hot sparks." He seemed a bit taken-back by my close guess at the nature of the metal.

"I originally trained as a chemist," I explained. "So, you strike the ferrocerium with the knife blade and you get sparks to start a fire?"

"Right. Like its name, it's mostly iron and cerium, but it also contains a few other metals, one of which is magnesium, like your first guess. The advantage is that you can make sparks even in cold, damp conditions. That makes it better than flint. Better yet is to use the knife to scrape some ferrocerium shavings onto some tinder then strike it to produce the sparks. Try practising it a few times and you'll never forget the trick."

"And I should tape it somewhere, just like with the gun?"

"Exactly, it's small, light, won't rust and could save your life. My father used to tell me to always carry a knife and to always carry a way to make a fire. I used to think it was a quaint old notion, but maybe the old advice still applies where you're going."

"Thank you, Scotty, I really appreciate this. You obviously kept these for a reason, are you sure you're willing to part with them?"

Sergeant Scott peered out at me again for a moment, from under his bushy eyebrows, and then shrugged. "I have two daughters that I'd never want anything bad to happen to" he said, pausing in thought... "I think maybe I kept them for you."

I was saved from having to come up with any kind of appropriate reply to this as he immediately turned, went back to the front of the armoury, and sat down at his desk. Selecting a form from a rack, he inserted it in to the typewriter and began to type while issuing a string of brusque questions: full name, regimental number, home address, and so on. Finishing one, he inserted another form and started typing on it as well. When he was done, he carefully tore the perforated tops off from each form, removed the carbon-copies from the backs, and handed the two originals over to me.

"Restricted weapons permits," he said. "These show that they were officially issued to you. If you lose the originals or need to clear yourself with other authorities, have someone call this office –

the copies will be on file right here."

As I turned to go, he added, "Do me one favour. When it's all over, come back and tell me what it was really all about, will you?"

"I promise, Scotty."

4 NOVA SCOTIA BOUND

I still had the big red and white '76 Chevy Cheyenne, 4-door crew-cab, pickup truck that I'd purchased when posted to Alberta the previous year. It was great for long road trips, and Silver always seemed highly amused by his ability to take over the back seat and alternate hanging his head out of the windows on each side. Any time that I teased him about this, he'd give me a big wolfly grin and one of his meaningful wide-eyed looks, that always made me wonder just how much of my thoughts and speech he actually understood.

Silver's cover story was easy. He was supposed to be my dog and best friend. That was true, although he and I were much closer than that – kind of like the brother that I'd never had. My cover story was a bit more complex.

"The fewer the number of people that know what you're up to when you're working on cases, the better. It improves your chances of success, and it's safer for you that way," Bob always insisted. We did have to bring a few people into our confidence, however.

Since the woman that had originally discovered the old weather station was a biochemist working in a Chemistry Department and given that contacting her would be one of my first tasks, Bob decided I should go back to my roots and go out as a chemist myself. This wasn't as much of a stretch as it might seem since I had originally trained at Carleton University to become an analytical chemist. Bob wanted my old analytical chemistry professor at Carleton to 'hire' me back as a Research Associate, and then send me out to Nova Scotia to study something that would require travelling around and taking samples, and therefore a good excuse to snoop around. I'd liked my prof at Carleton but wondered out loud why in the world he should agree to take me on to do an imaginary job that he probably wouldn't have any real interest in.

"Patriotism maybe?" Bob had replied, but the Cheshire Cat grin was back on his face. I had to laugh when I discovered the real answer, which was simplicity itself. Bob just offered him a healthy research grant, saying that the prof was free to use the money to do whatever kind of research he wanted, as long as he'd act the role of my employer and supervisor if anyone started asking questions.

"You know, to be fair, he might go along with all this for free," I'd suggested to Bob before the two of us had headed over to Carleton to broach the subject with my former prof.

"I'd like to think so," said Bob, "but this is a small price to pay to get his complete cooperation. If little annoyances should come up while you're out east, I want him fully on-board with us, and not irritated enough to make mistakes or opt out without warning."

My old prof, Dr. Alan Grey, had found the whole thing interesting and amusing, was very appreciative of the research grant and seemed genuinely taken with the notion of playing a small role in a 'cloak and dagger' affair, as he called it. With his help, we decided that I'd go out to collect samples for a study of possible connections between heavy metal concentrations and the 'Red Tide' phenomenon that occasionally played havoc with the East Coast fishery.

"Is there such a connection?" I'd asked. I knew about heavy metal analyses but not much biochemistry.

"Who knows? That's why they call it research!" said Dr. Grey. "Maybe there's an inverse correlation if the heavy metals are toxic to the algae." He paused, thinking it over. "Tell you what, let's make it a real research project and find out. If you're sampling before the Red Tide hits, then we'll say you're collecting baseline samples. If the Red Tide actually strikes while you're out there, then you'll take the comparison samples. We'll go ahead and analyze the samples back here and if we spot anything interesting, we might even be able to publish the results," he said, starting to smile his own kind of satisfied inner smile as the notion began to appeal to his professional interests.

So that settled the first part. Alex Houston, B.Sc. would re-enter the world of science.

***

Silver and I had a great trip driving from Ottawa to Halifax. The nine hundred-mile trip along the Trans-Canada Highway took us through Montreal to Quebec City, where we stopped overnight, and then through Fredericton and Moncton, New Brunswick, and from there to Truro, Nova Scotia. From Truro, it was only another hour's drive south to Halifax.

Our office staff in Ottawa had rented a nice, unassuming old house for us in Halifax. It had a small yard in the back, but it was large enough for me to park the truck there with about two-thirds left over for grass, on which Silver could roll around and play, and on which I could install a Bar-B-Que and a couple of chairs. We didn't need a lot of outdoor room for Silver, because the house was just off Robie Street, which put us only a block away from the Halifax Commons. If asked, I was to say that we'd gotten a great deal on the house from a local owner/investor that mostly just wanted the house lived-in and looked-after, while they waited for a hoped-for economic recovery that was supposed to drive prices up and create a selling opportunity. Nova Scotians always seemed to be waiting for an economic recovery that never seemed to materialize. Anyway, the idea was that with a house, I'd have enough room to deal with storing supplies and organizing all the samples I'd be collecting for shipment back to Ottawa.

The Commons is a large inner-city park. It is bounded on one side by a big hill, on top of which sits The Citadel, a partly restored 18th-century fortress. The Commons was a great place for Silver and I to go for runs and walks, and from there it was only a short distance to the downtown core and the harbour-front.

One of our favourite routes was to head up to the fortress, with its sweeping, panoramic views of the harbour, and then to drop down and stroll along the harbour-front area. As we discovered more of the city, another favourite became Point Pleasant Park, near the mouth of the harbour, which contains a virtual maze of harbour and forest pathways that were great for walks and runs.

Silver seemed to enjoy the city as much as I did, although he continued to display his curious habit of avoiding water. He didn't mind getting wet, so Halifax's frequent periods of fog and rain didn't bother him, but I could never coax him to jump into the ocean – not to walk and splash, not to chase a stick, and not even to join me in a refreshing swim (in Halifax, that's a euphemism for a freezing cold swim). It didn't bother me, and I could tell that there was something going on behind that penetrating gaze that he so often directed at me, but I simply filed it away in the back of my mind with the many other things I didn't understand about him.

Once Silver and I had settled in to the house and gotten our bearings in the city, it was time to approach Sharon at the university. I'd suggested simply contacting Sharon openly and directly, but Bob had vetoed that, feeling that she had no "need to know." In similar fashion, Bob didn't want me to approach his colleague at national defence or any of the crew from the Argus patrol aircraft, on the grounds that they'd already passed on everything they had, and they likewise had no need to know about Silver or me.

Instead, my Carleton prof had been asked to contact Sharon's Dal (Dalhousie University) professor, whom he knew slightly, and ask whether he could host me in his lab from spring through summer. My prof had relayed the gist of our research project and suggested that I'd only need occasional access to some lab bench and fume hood space in order to prepare my sample bottles and sampling reagents. Since we were going to be assaying samples for heavy metals back in Ottawa, I would need to carefully clean some of the sample bottles with an acid mixture, and I'd also need to treat some of the samples themselves with acids, and/or oxidizing or reducing media in order to preserve or change the oxidation states of the heavy metals in the samples. Sharon's prof, Dr. Ross Parke, had agreed, so that was my next destination.

Silver and I first did a walking reconnaissance of the Dal campus. As befits one of Canada's oldest cities, the Dal campus was beautiful and showed its age to advantage. Some of Canada's university campuses don't really stand out to the uninitiated observer as campuses, *per se*, in that they are so well distributed around the downtown cores of their respective host cities that one can't easily discern where the city ends, and the campus begins. Carleton and Dal's campuses appear more like the storybook image of universities, with fairly clear borders, a scattering of broad, treed grassy areas, and a heavy concentration of academic buildings of various sorts. That is where the similarities end though because whereas Carleton has a modern campus, with modern architecture, Dalhousie has an old-style campus. I don't mean this in a negative way. In fact, I found it charming. Its low stone fences, classical arrangement of ivy-covered brick buildings, and huge old trees created an old-world atmosphere that refused to be overwhelmed by the numerous more modern buildings that were tucked away here and there. Founded nearly 160 years previously, in 1818, Dal wore its age with style.

In the same vein, the two universities' Chemistry Buildings were certainly a study in contrasts. Whereas Carleton's was modern in every way, Dal's was a prime exemplar of its long history. I don't know whether the building was one of the first to have been built, but it certainly looked like it from the outside – a large, four-story brick building, covered in ivy and facing the campus's central quad area. It was flanked by the old Administration Building to one side, and by a massive, modern library on the other.

Having left Silver at home one day, while I went off for my first meeting with Dr. Parke, I found that the interior of the Chemistry Building didn't disappoint either. With its broad staircases, high ceilings, large pane-glass windows, and stately wooden doors and fittings, it struck me as the kind of building one might expect to find at Oxford or Cambridge in Britain, which I supposed made historical sense in a former British Colony.

Most of the faculty offices and research laboratories were on higher floors, and I eventually found Dr. Parke's office by the simple expedient of reading the name-plate on each door in turn. In this case, the office door was wide open, and the office itself unoccupied. Guessing that the nearest laboratory might be his, I tried walking in through its wide-open door and found a middle-aged man in rumpled clothes engaged in conversation with what was clearly a graduate student, or research assistant, of some kind. My first impressions of the lab itself were another contrast with the way I'd been trained. Beyond the sense of great space, with an impressively high ceiling, and equally impressive pane-glass windows, was wood! Wooden walls, wooden shelves, wooden lab benches, wooden fume hoods, and a hardwood floor!

I think it was the floor that dumbfounded me the most. At Carleton, I'd twice seen accidental mercury spills in the labs. Liquid metal mercury, that is, just like in a mercury thermometer but in larger quantities. Once spilled, the mercury would immediately break up into hundreds or thousands of tiny droplets and go racing off in all directions, reflecting light from their shiny, "silvery" surfaces. In this case, clean-up wasn't as difficult as you might imagine because the designers had foreseen this kind of accident and specified solid poured-epoxy floors that had no cracks and even curved upwards at the walls so that spilled liquids of any kind could be contained and dealt with. Not so in this lab, was my first thought. A mercury spill here would have all those little droplets speeding into the cracks between the hardwood slats and underneath the baseboards at the junctures with the walls. Realizing that the building itself was probably a hundred years old[17], I apprehensively wondered just how much mercury had fallen and accumulated 'between the cracks,' as it were, over all those years.

Such dark thoughts were quickly suspended when I heard a friendly "Hello!"

Introducing myself, I was immediately assured that this was, in fact, Dr. Parke's lab – he introduced himself, with a smile, as Ross, and then introduced me to his graduate student, who turned out to be Sharon Sanders.

"Wow, that was quick!" I thought to myself, appreciating the quick gift of a natural introduction to Sharon.

"Coffee?" Ross asked. Nodding in the affirmative, it took effort to keep my jaw from dropping at what came next.

Ross had picked up a coffee mug from the rack of pegs over the lab's main sink, where it had been nestled in among a variety of lab beakers and flasks that had presumably been cleaned and put up to dry. This was normal practice in many chemistry labs, as it avoided the possibility of contamination from cloth or paper drying towels. What wasn't normal, was having food or drink containers in the same place, or even in the lab at all.

This was only the beginning, however, as Ross took the coffee mug over to a central lab bench which I now saw was crowned by a large hollow glass figure of Obelix, a well-known comic book character[18]. The glass Obelix figure had been made in a classic pose with his body erect, his head lifted, and one arm raised about his shoulder. The hand of the raised arm held a large hollow war hammer, the head of which was positioned directly over a large filter funnel. The funnel had a cone of filter paper in it, and the filter paper must have held ground coffee because connected underneath the funnel was a large, inverted-cone-shaped Erlenmeyer flask sitting on the surface of a standard laboratory hot plate. Near the bottom of the flask, which was half-full of coffee, a small bent-glass tube led coffee to a rubber hose with a pinch-clamp. Placing the coffee mug under the rubber hose, Ross released the pinch-clamp to allow coffee to pour out, then closed it again, and turned to offer me the mug with a very nonchalant "Cream or sugar?"

He was a good actor, but the glint in his eyes gave him away. They were obviously very proud of their drip-coffee machine.

"Black is great thanks," I said, taking the mug. "Where in the world did you get this?"

"We have a very skilled scientific glassblower in the department. He makes all kinds of intricate glassware for us and, like our coffee machine here, he can make them out of Pyrex[19]."

I didn't even attempt to hide my amazement and, encouraged by this, he showed me how they filled and heated the water for it. A rubber hose was fitted to the side of the cartoon figure, with the other end connected to a lab-bench water tap, so that fresh water could be added by simply turning on the tap. As I watched, he turned on the tap and filled the figure half full of fresh water. The glass figure itself was clamped to the vertical post of a large ring-stand and held in place over the top of a Meker burner, which is basically a very high-heat version of the kind of natural gas-fuelled burners that you see in laboratories in movies or TV shows. A separate rubber hose led from the burner to the gas tap and placed very close to the top of the burner was the tip of an electrode.

It was Sharon's turn next.

"You're kidding," I exclaimed when she pointed to the electrode, but no, they weren't kidding. They had wired up the electrode to a high-voltage power supply, so that if you turned on the gas and then quickly punched a small push-button switch that was conveniently secured to the edge of the lab bench, a spark arced from the electrode the top of the burner, which ignited the gas to heat the water, which she briefly demonstrated. The high-intensity flame was directly below the glass figure's two hollow feet, and I could see that it would not take long to bring the water to a boil.

Ross was clearly pleased with my reactions to all this, saying, "Well, it's not all hard work and suffering around here."

I was pretty sure I was going to like these two, so I avoided making any comments about people that have watched too many 'mad scientist' movies. Besides, I was genuinely amazed and intrigued by their coffee machine. I kept my other surprise to myself, though. The lab culture here was very relaxed and friendly, which was a welcome contrast to the much more formal environment I had trained in at Carleton – but the safety standards were clearly more relaxed here as well. If any of us had been foolish enough to bring a cup of coffee into one of the labs there, much less make it, drink it, and clean and store the utensils in it, we'd have been figuratively taken out and shot! Similarly, whereas I'd trained in an atmosphere of mandatory lab coats, covered limbs and toes, and safety glasses, if not goggles, in this lab, it was T-shirts, shorts and sandals except when doing something that was clearly highly hazardous. "This was going to take some getting used to," I thought to myself, although I wasn't planning on spending much time in the lab.

Over coffee, I briefly reiterated the 'cover story' purpose of my arriving in Nova Scotia. This was news to Sharon but simply a repeat for Ross. I'd done some research on the Red Tide phenomenon before leaving Ottawa, and I gave them a summary of what I'd learned.

"I'm sure you two know more about the first part than me," I began, "but here goes. 'Red Tide' refers to periods of rapid marine algae growth, or 'blooms,' in which the algae can replicate themselves a million times in as little as two weeks. There are actually cycles of such growth, followed by decay periods, and the algae blooms usually occur in spring and summer when there are favourable conditions of light intensity and available nutrients in the ocean. The name itself comes from the fact that having many millions of coloured algae in the water causes the water to appear to take on their colour, the most common of which is red." Ross and Sharon nodded their heads. This, they knew.

"OK then, the public concern comes from the fact that some of these algae are poisonous for humans, but are eaten by filter-feeding shellfish, such as mussels, clams, and oysters. The toxins produced by the poisonous algae then accumulate in the shellfish. Depending on the strain and concentration of the toxins, the results of eating such contaminated shellfish have ranged from stomach upset and diarrhea, to amnesia, to paralysis, to death. To counter this threat, government agencies regularly monitor shellfish toxicity, and when they detect dangerous concentrations, they close the affected areas to shellfish harvesting. The reason that the government has to constantly do sampling and testing is that sometimes the Red Tide effect is severely toxic for humans, sometimes it's only mildly uncomfortable, and sometimes there is no noticeable effect on humans at all." Ross and Sharon kept nodding. This too, was familiar to them.

"So, people in your field are trying to work out whether it's a case of different strains of algae causing different effects, which is the conventional theory. Our team is interested in whether the toxic algae are sometimes being deactivated by heavy metals – either metals in the ocean itself, or metals that also concentrate in the shellfish. The idea is that certain metals, or maybe certain concentrations of certain metals, might be dampening or eliminating the toxic effects of the algae." I paused, expectantly, but they continued to nod their heads and simply asked me a few questions about which metals and which oxidation states we thought might be involved, and how we were going to analyze for them. This was more familiar territory for me, and I could hear my voice gain confidence as I listed some of the kinds and forms of heavy metals that, frankly, are almost always the ones of concern in any environmental chemistry issue, and the various methods and instruments we had in our labs for analyzing for them. This, we discussed a bit more over our coffees.

Thankfully, they seemed to accept my story at face value, didn't press me for many more details, and if they thought our research project was a bit of a shot in the dark, they were polite enough not to say so or to challenge me on it.

Getting down to the business at hand, Ross said that he'd just had a Ph.D. student graduate and was trying to find a new one to start in September. This meant that there was a vacant desk in the lab that I was welcome to use between then and now. It made for perfect timing for me, and I gratefully accepted and thanked him. Not only would this be convenient for my cover work, but it also made Sharon and I 'lab-mates,' or "fellow lab rats," as she called us, in keeping with the biological aspects of her own research project, which I was to learn about later.

Ross had provided me with an account number so that I could charge chemicals and sample bottles from the department's Stores, which was extremely helpful for me. He'd waved off my thanks, saying that it was no problem and that if the costs added-up to anything serious he'd just send my own prof a bill for them, but in any case, "Not to worry." This allowed me to get started right away, and for the rest of the week, I divided my time among getting things sorted out in the lab, getting to know Sharon and the campus, and getting to know Halifax.

I think my Fort McMurray yard-party experiences must have left a lasting impression on me because, although the rented house was officially fully-furnished, it was not furnished with a backyard Bar-B-Que. Accordingly, that became one of my first Halifax purchases. The only other thing a Bar-B-Que calls for is company, so by the end of that first week, I'd invited Sharon over for a Saturday dinner in my small backyard.

Sharon's arrival at my place marked her first introduction to Silver. She'd noticed my tendency to disappear every lunch-time during the week, and I'd explained that I went home every day to feed and visit with Silver, so he wasn't just stuck alone in the house by himself all day.

The topic of Silver's breed hadn't come up, as Sharon wasn't much into dogs, and I rather suspect that she imagined that he might be something small, like a Yorkie or possibly a Miniature Poodle. Sharon is quite petite, which may have had something to do with her ideas, but whatever she expected it wasn't what she met.

I hadn't heard her ring the front doorbell, although Silver clearly did, as his head immediately popped-up and he went into his high-alert, sensing mode. With my hands full, I couldn't head for the front door right away. Before I could break away to go to the door, Sharon had quite reasonably just walked around to the back of the house to see if we were there. She reached the fence gate just before Silver did, and the sight of what she first took to be a huge wolf bounding up caused her to take a big step back and raise her hands in the air with a loud "Whoa!"

For his part, Silver had given a single bark at her approach, and now was simply interested in seeing if she was going to pass his careful "sniff test," but Sharon didn't know that. She was initially reluctant to advance a step and hold out her hand for him to sniff, but with some encouragement from me, gathered up her courage and gave it a try. She quickly relaxed, however, after Silver gave her a series of deep sniffs, took a long, deep gaze into her eyes and then, satisfied, gave her hand a quick lick. Only then did he turn to look at me in a meaningful way that seemed to say, "This one's OK." It never ceased to amaze me how his penetrating looks seemed to plant message-images in my head.

With Silver's approval having been granted, we poured ourselves drinks, water for Silver and wine for Sharon and I, and settled into a great dinner and evening of visiting. By the end of the evening I couldn't help but smile as I noticed that the two of them were comfortably sitting together on the sofa, Silver curled up with his back nestled against her leg, and Sharon unconsciously stroking his fur with her left hand. "That didn't take long," I thought to myself, wondering which of them was actually the larger and heavier. I suspected it might be Silver, but it didn't matter as Sharon had quickly gotten over her first apprehensions, and they'd already become friends.

Our evening discussions covered a range of topics including Sharon's research project, which involved chemical interactions between seawater and ocean sediments, and was a combination of chemistry, biochemistry, and chemical oceanography. As she described her research Sharon mentioned, in passing, that she was going to need to plan a few dives to get water and sediment samples from a few locations.

Discovering in this way that we both had an interest in SCUBA diving sparked an entire discussion about freshwater diving (which was all I'd done to that point) and saltwater diving (which was all Sharon had done). It further came out that Sharon didn't have any regular dive buddies, but simply joined the university SCUBA club when they planned group outings. Sensing an unstated plea for help, I volunteered to go and help with her sampling if she wanted. It was the right thing to say as she gave me a huge smile and gratefully accepted.

I had left my diving gear with my parents in Ottawa, so the next day I called and asked them to ship it all out by air cargo the following week.

5 EAST COAST DIVING

The following weekend, Sharon was visiting Silver and I in the backyard of my house again, this time examining my SCUBA gear. Sharon approved everything that I had but warned me that I'd need to add a couple of pounds of lead weight to my weight belt to allow for the increased buoyancy I'd have in saltwater versus the freshwater that I'd been used to.

Since I'd never been in the ocean before, we decided that Sharon would take me out for an orientation dive before we started on any sample-collecting dives for her.

"Can we go see a shipwreck?" I asked.

"That's easy," Sharon laughed. "There are more shipwrecks per mile of coastline here than anywhere else in the world. Partly because of all the wars, from the war with the Americans in 1812, all the way through the First and Second World Wars, and there are more recent wrecks too."

"Sounds exciting!" I exclaimed, my imagination taking off.

Seeing this, Sharon felt compelled to lower my expectations a bit, saying, "I should tell you that most of the wrecks look more like junk yards than ships. It's not just because of their age, though. The pounding of rough seas against wrecks that are up against big rocks means that even modern wrecks get torn to shreds very quickly."

"They're still worth seeing though," Sharon hastily added, seeing my face drop.

Sharon suggested that we start with the wreck of the Humboldt,

45

and that's where we found ourselves a week later.

The nice thing about diving in Nova Scotia is that there are so many great spots that can be reached by hiking, rather than requiring a boat. The not so nice thing is that those hikes always seem to be over rough terrain, and they often involve hiking down narrow pathways from a cliff, and all this while carrying all the diving gear: compressed air tank, regulator, gauges, mask, snorkel, fins, diving knife, full wetsuit, weight belt with twenty pounds of lead weights, towel, plus a thermos of something hot, for later.

As we were finally getting our gear assembled near the water's edge, we could at least appreciate that we'd picked a fine day for diving. The sky was clear, with only the occasional cloud, and there was very little wind. This meant that the ocean, for once, was calm, with only a gentle swell causing small waves to break-up on the near-shore rocks. The water itself was a deep blue colour in the distance, but a lighter, greenish blue near the shore – indicating that the sediment below was unlikely to have been recently stirred-up, and underwater visibility should be quite good.

During the preceding week, Sharon had brought a book on local shipwrecks in to the lab. According to the book, the Humboldt had been an American steam-driven, paddle-wheel ocean liner. On December 5, 1853, it had been crossing the Atlantic Ocean, on its way from Southampton to New York, when rough weather and a shortage of coal had apparently led its captain to decide to divert to Halifax. Unfortunately, they never made it. Hampered by poor visibility, the ship ran aground on shoals near Sambro Island. They were able to get the ship off the rocks, but that only delayed the inevitable as it was rapidly taking on water. The captain then purposely ran the ship aground in Portuguese Cove, just twelve miles south of Halifax, in an attempt to save the lives of the ninety passengers and crew. Although all but one of the people on board were saved, the ship was torn apart by intense waves and sank, along with most of its cargo. Now, I was going to observe what was left of the wreck, over 120 years later.

We geared up and I told Silver that I would be back soon and that he should stay near our gear bags on the shore and wait for us. As always, he showed absolutely zero interest in going anywhere near the water. Also, as always, he seemed to understand what I was asking him to do. I took both for granted, but Sharon thought that both were very odd.

"I don't know which is stranger," she remarked, looking at us. "I've never heard of a large dog being afraid of the water before, and I can't get over how you two seem to be able to actually communicate with each other."

"I think something must have happened to him when he was younger, to make him dislike going in the water, but I can't imagine what it would have been," I replied.

"We have always been able to understand each other though," I added, thoughtfully. "If I speak slowly and carefully, and directly to him, he seems to be able to get a sense of what I'm thinking, even if he only understands a few of the actual words. I don't usually talk about it because I used to think that I didn't believe in psychic things – it goes against my scientific training and instincts after all. Another reason is that I don't want people to think I'm crazy, ... but there's something there all the same. It works both ways, too. Sometimes he'll give me that penetrating stare of his, and I'll get a sense in my mind of what he's thinking. More like pictures or emotions than words, but very real. He saved my life that way once, and it happens so often between the two of us that I tend to take it for granted now. Please keep it to yourself, OK?"

"Fine with me," Sharon agreed. "Whatever it is, it's pretty cool."

With a last word of reminder to Silver, we carefully entered the water with all our gear on, excepting our fins. The cold water immediately began to work its way through our wetsuits. That hit me like a shock wave, and I chomped down on the mouthpiece of my snorkel as I waited out the few minutes it took for my body heat to warm the water to something reasonable, if not comfortable.

Once we were past most of the big rocks, we donned our fins and moved to slightly deeper water, so I could test my buoyancy. I mentioned earlier that Sharon had recommended an adjustment to my weight belt to compensate for the increased buoyancy of seawater over the freshwater that I'd been used to. I'd added just a bit too much weight and compensated for it by releasing a bit of air into my buoyancy compensator[20] – which is like an inflatable life vest, but more sophisticated and with a compressed air line and a dump-valve, so air could be easily added or released as needed. Later, I would note all this in my dive log and reduce the weight on my belt for the next dive.

Finally, ready to proceed, Sharon showed me the landmarks on the shore that local divers used to estimate their heading to the wreck site, and with these in mind, we headed for deeper water. To save air, we snorkeled out for a while before switching to our regulators and diving down. I don't know how much of it was following Sharon's bearings and how much just good luck, but we found the right spot almost right away. As we descended the water colour shifted from greenish blue to blue, and as we crossed the thermocline at just over 30 feet of depth, the water instantly became much colder and a darker blue.

We found part of the wreck at a depth of 40 feet – with several ribs from the hull and some long spikes sticking up from the bottom. Continuing to follow the downward slope of the ocean floor we soon found what the local divers called the 'Button Hole,' at a depth of 50 feet. At this depth, there was much less light. Everything was rendered in shades of dark blue, but the visibility was still pretty good. Pretty good that is, until we started to stir up the sediment.

Sharon motioned me to dig around in the sand, in between the rocks and boulders, and sure enough, I found several buttons and nails. The digging stirred up a cloud of fine-grained sediment, however, and I soon couldn't see a thing in front of me. I kept on searching, though, working by feel alone, and I was rewarded by finding a few more things. Lifting a few feet off the bottom took me out of the sediment cloud and, able to see again, I found that I'd been rewarded by finding a couple of small, shiny medallions or charms of some kind. I'd never found artifacts on a shipwreck before and didn't want to lose them, so I slipped them one by one under the cuff and into my left wetsuit mitt, having nowhere else to put them.

Looking up, I caught Sharon's eyes and waved my pressure gauge at her. She used her hands and fins to move closer to me, so we could see each other's gauges. Mine read 900 psi, while hers read 1500psi. "Damn," I thought, "she's in better diving shape than I am!" On second thought though, this had been my first ocean dive so maybe I was entitled to a bit faster air consumption. In any case, low pressure meant time to head back and I gave the 'let's go up' hand signal to her. She nodded agreement and we slowly ascended straight up.

Breaking the surface and inflating my buoyancy compensator to keep me floating with my head up, I saw that we were now quite far from shore. Sharon had warned me to save more reserve air than I would have done in fresh water diving. She explained that it was common to surface from a dive to find that the sea was rougher than it had been when we entered, and it could make life a lot easier if we had enough air left to use our regulators rather than have to revert to snorkels.

"Why?" I'd asked, naively.

"If the sea is rough, we'll have waves crashing over our heads every once in a while. It's no fun having a wave push your head under water and then fill your snorkel to boot. The first time isn't so bad, but pretty soon you get very tired and you'll need your energy to watch the waves as we near the shore, so we can make the final dash for shore in between wave crests. Otherwise, we get slammed into the rocks for good measure.

This prompted me to retort "Why are we doing this again?" but she knew that I was joking.

As it turned out, we were lucky on this day, as the sea was just as beautifully tranquil as it had been when we first entered the water. Nevertheless, it was a long swim back. On top of that we were now both becoming chilled from the cold water, and tired from our exertions, and it really was easier to be able to keep breathing air from my regulator than from my snorkel.

The relatively calm sea made exiting the water easy as well, and we were soon carrying our gear back to where Silver had been lying in comfort across our two large gear bags. Our adventure wasn't quite over yet, though. Coming out of the water chilled and tired, I was surprised at the additional chill contributed by the moist, onshore wind that had come up from out of nowhere. This, however, I was prepared for. Unzipping my huge gear bag, I quickly extracted a blanket into which I'd long ago cut a head-sized hole, right in the centre. Pulling it over my head created a kind of tent that blocked the wind and absorbed some of the water while I stripped off the rest of my wetsuit and my bathing suit. As I started to use my towel to dry myself off, under the blanket, I heard a sharp exclamation from Sharon.

"Where in the world did you get that?" she asked, sounding amazed.

"I made it myself, from an old blanket," I replied, still towelling myself vigorously. "When I was diving in Ontario and Quebec, it was generally with one of two other girls and a bunch of guys. The blanket-poncho idea was originally just for privacy while changing, but my first winter ice-dive in an old Quebec limestone quarry taught me that it was a great way to warm up too. Now, I've just learned that it also makes a great wind break. When we get back to town we can make you one too."

"Thank you, that would be so great." Sharon seemed genuinely appreciative of such a small thing, and I realized that sharing a lab and a first adventure together were bringing us close together. This provoked a flash of shame that I was in Nova Scotia under false pretenses, and even as I immediately suppressed such thoughts I already knew deep down that I was going to have to tell her at least some of the truth before long.

"Not yet," though, I told myself as I dug into my dive bag for my final surprise. Pulling out a thermos flask, with its cup-lid and a spare cup, I quickly filled each cup and passed one over to her. "Try this now, but carefully – it's very hot" was all I said.

Taking the steaming cup from my hand, Sharon sniffed at it suspiciously and then tried a sip. "Wow, that's hot," and then, after a second sip, "what is this stuff? It's tomato soup, but something's different about it."

"You got it. Hot cream of tomato soup with powdered red pepper added. It's hot from the heat, loaded with calories, and the red peppers make it taste hotter than it really is. Some of the hot taste is an illusion, but when I'm really cold I find that it works for me."

"Me too," said Sharon draining her cup at a rate that should have burned her mouth and tongue. "Got any more?"

Laughing, I poured her another cup.

Warmer now, we chatted about the dive as we finished changing into dry clothes. Finally, armed with our last cup of hot soup, we sat on our filled dive bags and filled out our dive logs: average depth 40 feet, maximum depth 50 feet, visibility 30 feet (vertical) and 15 to 30 feet (horizontal), air pressure in: 3100 psi, pressure out: 900 psi, and total bottom time[21] 60 minutes.

"Not bad at all," I thought. Out loud, I said, "I'm surprised that there are still buttons and things to be found in the sand if this is such a popular diving spot."

"That's partly why the 'Button Hole' is famous among divers around here. Apparently, the ship was carrying a fortune in dry goods and a lot of stuff just happened to sink into that nice little spot where it is protected on all sides by lots of big rocks. Also, the storms churn up the bottom, so every once in a while, a fresh batch of things to find seems to get churned up. It has to run out someday, but it hasn't yet. Did I see you finding some things down there?' she asked.

"I did," I said excitedly and emptied my wetsuit mitt into one hand to show her. "I found some buttons and nails, and some kind of medallions or charms."

Taking them into her hand for a closer look, she said "These aren't jewelry; they're pocket watch winding keys. Most people, certainly most men, had pocket watches in 1853, and at that time most of them had to be wound with a separate key. The keys were usually attached to the pocket watch chain, so they wouldn't get lost, and they were often decorated to look nice when hanging on the chain." Then, peering more closely, "I think these are brass. If so, they'll look really nice if you polish them up."

"Did you find anything down there?" I asked, suddenly concerned that I might have had all the fun of discovery.

"Just one thing," she said mysteriously. Nonchalantly, she then up-ended a wetsuit glove, and out fell ..."

"A pocket watch cover," I exclaimed.

"Look again," she retorted.

Taking the cover, I turned it over. "I think it's the whole watch," I said, amazed. "Are you going to open it?"

"Not here," replied Sharon, "I'm going to soak it in distilled water for a few days when we get back to the lab, and then I'll dry it and take it to a watch repair shop," and then, after a pause, she added the clincher: "I think it might be gold."

"Gold!"

"I'm not sure, but I've seen a lot of brass come up from shipwrecks and this looks shinier to me. Anyway, gold or brass, I'm going to get it cleaned up either way. If it can't be fixed, then I'll get it mounted so it can sit on a shelf or mantelpiece."

There was one final chapter to this adventure, and that came as we were just finishing our gear packing and getting ready for the trek back to my truck.

"By the way," Sharon asked, "when we were following the bottom to the Button Hole, why did you keep turning to look behind you? It wasn't to keep an eye on me because I was right beside you."

"Oh that," I looked at her directly, but I felt the flush of my cheeks reddening, "I was hoping you hadn't noticed that."

"What gives?"

"I'm embarrassed to admit this, but here goes ... do you remember how the Spielberg movie *Jaws* was the big movie to see when it came out two years ago?"

"No!" she exclaimed, but she clearly did remember and meant no to what I was about to admit.

"Yes!" I nodded, "you remember how the great white shark terrorized a small American town?" She nodded. "And the shark was huge?" More nods. "And in the movie, there'd be this thumping music that would slowly increase in volume, and then the shark would suddenly loom right out of the dark blue water to attack people?"

Sharon was still nodding, her mouth open. She knew what was coming now.

"Well, this was my first experience diving in the ocean, and there we were at 50 feet down, suddenly surrounded by dark, blue water, and in the back of my mind I imagined I could hear that music again, and I kept involuntarily looking over my shoulder ..."

"Trying to spot the shark," Sharon finished for me.

She didn't say a thing at first. I expected her to laugh and make a joke, but she surprised me by dropping her gear bag and coming close, so she could give me a big hug. Now, I'm not generally big on hugs, but Sharon's instinctive warmth really touched me, as did the hug itself.

"I would never have thought of that," she said, "maybe I'm not the imaginative type. But I understand fear well enough. My first check-out dives after SCUBA training were in the ocean and on the first two I was terrified the whole time. If we hadn't been required to do three check-out dives, and if I hadn't been too stubborn to back out of a dive I'd already paid for I probably wouldn't have even gone in for the third dive. I was lucky I did though, because everything finally went right for me on the third dive, and I learned to get over my fears and enjoy diving on that one 'last' dive. So there – we're even on embarrassing stories."

"For now," I laughed, as we picked up our gear and walked with Silver back to my truck for the drive back to Halifax and my sort-of home. Silver had seemed to pay close attention to our exchange of stories, and emotions, and it seemed to somehow draw he and Sharon closer together as well. Driving back to town, I noticed that he'd abandoned his traditional habit of commanding the back seat and had instead planted himself firmly in Sharon's lap where he promptly fell into a doze, likely aided by Sharon's constant, gentle stroking of his fur.

The driving and a companionable silence got me back to thinking about my mission. The diving had been a great change of pace, and now I had to help Sharon with some dives of her own, but with a fresh new week around the corner, I was also going to have to find a way to check out the Cape Breton discovery that had led to my real assignment.

***

In the week that followed, I found that I was able to combine helping Sharon with dives she needed to make for her research project with collecting samples for my own cover-story research project. Sharon had picked three sites for her work, one down south by Lunenburg, one near Peggy's Cove, and one – I couldn't believe my luck – in Cape Breton. All three were beautiful and historic locations that made for great sight-seeing while we were there. The Lunenburg dive was uneventful, and we each collected the samples we needed without difficulty. Getting the water samples was easy, Sharon needed some sediment samples from a moderate depth, so I grabbed a couple for myself, just in case they might be useful later, and Sharon helped me find a few mussels and clams which we shucked on the spot since I didn't need the shells.

The dive near Peggy's Cove was a bit more exciting.

The dive site Sharon had selected wasn't literally Peggy's Cove, the famous tourist site, but about a mile away, at a spot called Polly's Cove. Whereas Peggy's Cove was well marked with huge signs aimed at inviting the tourists, Polly's Cove is completely unmarked. Fortunately, Sharon knew where she was going and directed me onto an almost invisible dirt road that shortly came to an abrupt stop in front of boulders that were nearly the size of my truck. From there we had to hike with our gear, and our bags of sample bottles, along an almost imperceptible trail that led along a tall cliff.

Compared to the great weather and calm seas of our previous two dives, this day looked miserable. It was cloudy and grey with a touch of fog, plus a light drizzle that made the rocks wet and slippery. As we marched along the top of the cliff, I could see that the sea was quite rough, with lots of whitecaps in evidence. Sharon seemed quite unconcerned about all this, however. I'd learned that her judgement was sound, so Silver and I followed along.

One thing that Polly's Cove and Peggy's Cove had in common were incredible views of Nova Scotia's rugged coastline beauty. The only thing preventing it from being a potentially favourite hike was that we soon had to carefully make our way along a series of switchbacks as the path led down to the ocean. Going down was hard enough; I wasn't looking forward to the return trip!

As we followed the path down to the water I learned why Sharon hadn't been worried about the rough sea. Polly's Cove is a small cove that is well protected by a long, curving spit of rock, forming a natural breakwater. On the seaward side, we could see water being constantly thrown up as waves hammered into the rocks, but on the landward side, the water was relatively calm, with only a gentle swell rising and falling. As we paused about halfway down, to catch our breath, Sharon explained that the Hulda had broken up over the spit of rock, leaving about half of the wreck lying in the sheltered part and about half lying on the seaward side. It was near high tide when we got there, but Sharon said that at low tide part of the wreck could be seen projecting out of the water. Despite the miserable weather, I couldn't help admiring the dive site: a naturally protected cove with part of a shipwreck neatly provided in its care. Sharon said I should expect to see lots of marine life taking shelter in and around the wreck.

As we sat on the path to rest, Sharon pulled out a photocopy of a few pages from her book of Nova Scotia shipwreck descriptions and began to read aloud. Compared with the 120-year-old Humboldt that we'd visited the previous week, this was a much more recent wreck. A small cargo ship, the Hulda had run aground on the curving spit of rock almost exactly six years previously. That is, in late May of 1971. Since the ship had been damaged beyond recovery, everything that was considered salvageable was removed from the ship over the following several months, leaving the remnants for divers and marine life alike to enjoy.

Having rested, we gathered up our gear and finished our hike down to the water's edge. In what was now our standard pattern, we checked and donned our gear, I asked Silver to stay and wait for us, and we carefully made our way into the water. Finding the wreck was easy, we simply snorkeled to the centre of the cove, switched to regulators, dove for the bottom, and there it was.

Work was our top priority, so we first collected our water and sediment samples, and then Sharon once again helped me to find some shellfish. Just mussels this time, but that was enough for me, I thought. We had each brought rope-mesh bags with us to carry our sample bottles in, and our filled sample bottles and my shellfish out. Once they were filled, we used a piece of rope to tie them together and connect them to a small inflatable lift-bag that Sharon always kept attached to her weight belt. She held the lift-bag with its open end facing down, clipped the rope to a set of straps that hung down from the bag, then filled the lift-bag with air by holding her regulator under the open end and depressing the constant-flow button of her regulator. Once the bag was about two-thirds full of air, she released it and it shot up to the surface to wait for us at the end of our dive.

Now that the work part was over, we still had lots of compressed air left for an exploration of the wreck, which lay upright on the bottom, at a depth of about 40 feet. Some of the ship's compartments had been cut and/or torn wide open so that two divers could enter together and without fear of becoming trapped inside the wreck. It quickly became obvious that it was the stern half of the ship, as we found ourselves in what was left of the engine room. Leaving the engine room and swimming a circuit around the outside of the wreck showed us a variety of unrecognizable, rusting machinery scattered here and there.

It was cold and impending tiredness this time, rather than low air pressure, that caused us to halt our explorations and ascend to the surface. As we did, I mentally compiled the vital statistics that I'd later enter into my dive log: average and maximum depth both 40 feet, visibility 30 feet (vertical and horizontal), air pressure in: 3200 psi, pressure out: 1400 psi, and total bottom time 40 minutes. Another great dive, I thought, and Sharon had been right about the marine life: I'd seen lots of ocean perch, sea anemones of different colours, and even a couple of crabs lying on the bottom watching me to see whether they'd need to scuttle away or not.

Once we'd surfaced, we spotted Sharon's bright orange lift

bag floating nearby, collected it and our samples and turned to swim for shore thinking our adventure for the day was complete.

Except that it wasn't.

At the same time as we were retrieving our sample bags, I could hear the sound of Silver barking at someone who was standing on the beach not far from our gear bags. We had to first focus on reaching the shore, getting our fins off, and dragging our bags of samples up out of the water. As soon as we had that accomplished, I could see that Silver had been barking at a very angry looking, elderly man that could only have been a fisherman.

As I looked more closely at the man, he raised his left arm and with it a double-barreled shotgun that he had been holding out of our sight behind his left leg. As I softly called Sharon's name to get her attention, she raised her eyes from what she'd been doing to join me in the uncomfortable position of looking at the muzzle of the shotgun.

"What the hell do you two think you're doing raiding my traps?" the man asked.

"Traps?" I asked, genuinely puzzled.

"He means lobster traps, Alex," explained Sharon. "He thinks we've been raiding his lobster traps." Then, speaking to the angry man, "Look, mister, we haven't touched your traps. We're scientists, collecting water and sediment samples. If you put that gun down, we'll show you."

"Not so fast," retorted the fisherman, "I don't trust city people."

By this time, I was getting concerned, not because I was afraid that this guy was going to shoot us, but because I could see that Silver had been carefully watching this guy and was now slinking along in a flanking maneuver. Any moment now he was going to be in a position that was just outside of the fisherman's peripheral vision, but within range for a leap for the arm that was attached to his trigger finger. He'd been trained not to disarm a suspect until I gave the command, but I wasn't sure he'd heed that training if he thought I was in imminent danger.

"Please," I added my voice to Sharon's, "Put the gun down and give us a chance to convince you that we're innocent."

The fisherman still looked angry, did not at all seem disposed to listen to us, was still pointing the shotgun at us, and at fairly close range too. I knew what a shotgun could do to us at that range, and

I didn't like our odds if his trigger finger got shaky. I was debating whether to identify Silver as a police dog and warn him that he might have more to fear from Silver than we did from him, but I had an uneasy feeling that I wouldn't be believed and also that he might just turn and shoot Silver first, leaving a second barrel ready for us.

Fortunately, I was saved from making a final decision by a loud, commanding voice that suddenly filled the air.

"That's enough of that Angus. Put the gun down." This from a largish man, in some kind of uniform, who was picking his way toward us over and around the rocks.

The fisherman obviously knew this voice, because he immediately lowered his weapon and turned to face the newcomer. "I'm in the right, Stephen. I've a right to protect my traps."

"That's right, Angus, you do, although I don't think a judge would think you were justified in shooting two unarmed girls even if they did disturb your traps ... do you?"

"Girls?" said the fisherman, his anger turning to amazement.

"Girls," said the uniformed man definitively. "Listen to their voices and, if you'll pardon me, ladies, look at the curve of their hips!"

Trying to play along, Sharon and I both pulled off our wetsuit hoods and shook our hair out, emphasizing our gender.

"Well, I don't hear or see so well anymore," grumbled the fisherman sounding, and looking, confused.

"What do you say we have a look at what's in their catch-bags, hmmm? That should clear things up one way or the other." As he was saying this he purposefully strode over to our catch-bags, grabbed one end, and looked up at Sharon and me.

"Go ahead," we said, nearly in unison. I could see now that his uniform identified him as a Fisheries Officer.

Separating the bags from the rope he opened and fished around in each one with his hand. Then, setting them both back down on the sand he straightened up and looked over to the fisherman.

"Well, Angus, I see bottles of water, bottles of sand, and a handful of mussels, but I don't see any stolen lobsters. Do you want to come see for yourself?"

"No, not if you say so," grumbled the fisherman, subdued now and almost shuffling his feet.

"Well then, why don't we walk back up together and you can

buy me a rum and coke?"

The fisherman's reply was lost in the wind, but he shuffled around and started back up the path to the top of the cliff.

Stephen, the Fisheries Officer, then turned to us and said, "Sorry about Angus. The fishermen around here have had several incidences of sport divers stealing lobsters out of their traps, and it's making them cranky. That's no excuse for pointing a gun at you, even if – as I suspect – it wasn't loaded, but they're trying to protect their livelihood."

"Thank you for coming to our rescue," Sharon said. "We're sure glad you came along when you did."

"I don't think Angus would have done you any harm, but when I saw him headed this way with his shotgun, I had a feeling he was going to cause trouble. I'm glad you weren't taking any lobsters though because although I wouldn't have let him shoot you, I would have had to charge you. Under the new regulations, taking lobsters without a licence carries a hefty fine and confiscation of all your diving gear. You're welcome to the mussels though, no matter what you want them for."

Bidding us a good day, the Fisheries Officer turned up the trail, presumably to collect his unofficial fine of a glass of rum from the fisherman and leaving us to pack up.

"That felt like a close one," remarked Sharon, "but you seemed more concerned about Silver than yourself. Was I seeing things, or was he positioning himself to attack that guy before he could shoot?"

"It's a long story," I sighed. Things were getting complicated. "Would you be willing to trust me to tell you about it sometime, but just not right now?" I asked.

"A mystery woman," Sharon shrewdly observed. "OK, fine, but you have to promise to tell me eventually."

"I promise," was all I could say.

6 CAPE BRETON ISLAND

Cape Breton may or may not really be an island anymore, depending on your point of view. It once was an island, of course, being completely surrounded by water and requiring a ferry trip to get to mainland Nova Scotia. Between 1952 and 1955, however, a land-bridge, called the Canso Causeway, had been constructed to create a more efficient, higher traffic-volume, all-weather connection. It was still technically an island, because a narrow canal (the Canso Canal), with a swing-bridge, had been included to allow ship traffic to pass through. To the older generations, however, the land-bridge had turned the island into a peninsula.

Shortly after crossing the Causeway, the highway began to more closely follow the coastline and I was exposed to the incredible beauty and scenic vistas of the Cabot Trail.

When I had been briefly posted to Innisfail, Alberta the previous year[22], we had been so close to the Rocky Mountains that it had seemed natural for Silver and I to head off to explore them almost every weekend, and especially any time we had the opportunity of a three-day weekend. This had introduced us to what I thought must be the most beautiful highway drive in all of Canada: the Columbia Icefields Parkway. This judgement was severely tested by the beauty of the Cabot Trail, with its winding path alternating between forests and ocean-side vistas, and with the excitement that comes with a coastal highway that your left-brain (the rational, logical side) tells you must be safe, but your right-brain (the colourful and more interesting emotional side) keeps telling you is way too close to the edge, especially when, as often happens, the edge of the road is also the edge of a very high cliff above the ocean. Setting aside the meaningless debate about which drive was the more beautiful, I quickly resolved that I would come

back to Cape Breton and explore it further.
  Little did I know.

***

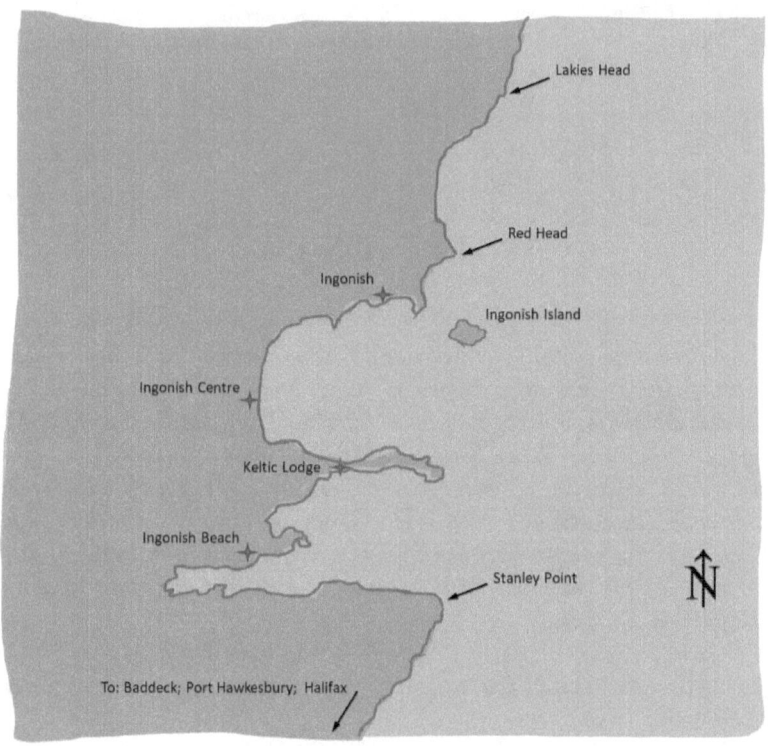

I think I read somewhere that you have to make choices as you proceed along life's journey, that there are seldom easy answers, and that you need to make the best choices that you can in the circumstances, and then move on and hope for the best. My next choice had to do with Sharon.

My instructions had been clear. What I was supposed to do was to find a way to get her to either describe for me or actually guide me to, the location of the mysterious apparatus she'd discovered on her Cape Breton hike the previous month. How I was supposed to pull that off without revealing my true identity or mission was up to me.

The problem was my conscience. Sharon had been so open, so helpful, and such a good friend, that I just couldn't keep on deceiving her. So, I decided to take the risk of filling her in.

Maybe the real lesson for me was that I just wasn't cut out for undercover work. I hadn't liked deceiving people when I'd been undercover in Fort McMurray[22], and I was even less happy about it now in Nova Scotia. In the end, I resolved that if I survived this mission, I'd tell Bob about it and take the consequences, but for now, I'd bring Sharon 'into the fold.'

So, it was a few days later, on the first Saturday of June, that Sharon was over for another of my backyard Bar-B-Ques. While she was playing with Silver, and I was tending to the grill, I told her the truth about me being a Mountie and Silver being a police dog, and that we'd been sent to follow-up on her strange discovery that she'd mentioned to her prof who had, in turn, contacted his colleague at National Defense.

Sharon hadn't been as surprised about Silver's and my real identities as she was that anyone thought her discovery was worth following up on. Although she was keen to see my badge and Silver's ID. I explained that a Canadian Forces Argus patrol aircraft had picked up unusual radio signals from roughly the same location just a month before she had made her discovery. The radio technician on the patrol aircraft had thought the signals were strange enough to send a copy to Dr. Keen at the Defence Research labs in Dartmouth. Dr. Keen, in turn, had been struck by the coincidence of the location being essentially the same as the one Sharon's supervisor had reported to him, and so he'd sent everything off to my boss in the RCMP Security Service. My boss thought it was worth following up on, hence Silver and I were snooping around.

Sharon whistled softly, "That's quite a chain of coincidences and suspicions! What makes it a police business? ... Wait, don't tell me. It's got to be spies? Right?"

Now I was starting to appreciate Bob's instructions about secrecy and questioning the wisdom of bringing Sharon into the loop. It was difficult to tell only part of a story, especially an interesting story. "In for a penny..." I thought to myself. Out loud I said, "It might be nothing, but if it *is* something, then it could be part of a covert messaging system for some kind of illegal activity. That probably means either organized crime or espionage."

"Does that really happen in Canada?"

"Organized crime, yes, constantly. Espionage, yes, sometimes. Not often, but sometimes."

"So, what do we do next?"

"We?" I responded. "There's no we. If you'll draw me a sketch-map and write out some directions, Silver and I will go check it out."

"I think I should come along and show you," Sharon asserted. "There shouldn't be any danger, right? No one else knows why you're here, and if we do run into anyone we'll just be two girls and a dog out for a day-hike, just like the thousands of tourists that swarm all over the province this time of year."

"Besides," she said, with a flash of inspiration, "with me along, I can arrange for our hike to take us directly to the site. Without me, you and Silver will have to search around to find it, and *that* would look suspicious, right?"

I had to laugh at her plotting. "All right, all right, you win. We'll go together. When could we go?"

"Tomorrow's Sunday. What better day for a day hike in Cape Breton?"

So, it was agreed, and as I already mentioned, the beautiful drive along Cape Breton's Cabot Trail almost made me forget why we were really there. Not completely, of course, but almost.

Although I agreed with Sharon that there wouldn't be much danger for the three of us doing the first reconnaissance, I'd taken the precaution of going armed. Since we were going to be hiking in T-shirts and shorts, I tried Scotty's suggestion of taping my Derringer and UDT knife to my inner thighs. With their lowest points about three inches above my knees, they were well hidden behind the Bermuda-style shorts that I was wearing. I had done some experimenting on previous weekends and found that they wouldn't stay in place if simply applied tape like for a bandage on a cut. Instead, I had to wrap the tape around my leg multiple times; more like you might with a small splint. It turned out that regular first-aid tape worked well but hurt like hell when it was removed. On the other hand, most other tapes didn't hurt coming off but didn't hold well either. Eventually, I did what I should have done in the first place: I went and asked a pharmacist for advice on tape for fragile skin. The pharmacist had suggested a kind of sensitive-skin tape that he said provided good adhesion, relatively pain-free removal, water resistance, and best of all, tears easily by hand. I tried it out, including in the shower, and it was perfect.

Just like Sharon had done on her earlier trip, we stopped at the Keltic Lodge resort for lunch (take-out, so we could eat outside, with Silver). On her advice, we had booked a cabin to share, near Ingonish Beach. Being early June, we were still in what was considered low season so the cost was reasonable, and Silver was allowed in the cabin (the real influx of tourists would begin just before the July long weekend). After checking in to the cabin, we drove north, past Ingonish, to the same place Sharon had previously parked off to the side of the highway. Although we wouldn't need them, we each put on a small backpack and Sharon took out her topographic map of the area. Sharon had already told me about the indistinct trail that she thought might be a game trail, and she now knew where it came out, so that's where we headed.

The one mile hike must have been a lot easier for us than Sharon's original bush-whacking and somewhat meandering route, and we made good time getting to the cliff at Red Head. Just like Sharon had described, all of a sudden, the forest came to an abrupt halt about twenty feet from the edge of the cliff. The cliff itself was about a hundred feet above sea level, and it offered quite stunning views of the ocean and of the coastline in both directions.

Like me, Sharon was on a mission, however, and she immediately said, "Over here!" and led me to the spot where she'd previously tripped over a rusty length of stranded wire rope attached to the top of a metal stake in the ground. Continuing past the stake, she pointed proudly at the strange assortment of rusty metal canisters and the two masts.

"Wow," I said, stepping carefully in among the tall grasses and bushes that were overgrowing the site.

"Do you know what it is?' Sharon asked.

"Well, I know what it was. It was an automatic weather station placed here by the German navy during the Second World War. Another one was found in Labrador earlier this year, and when it was taken apart, our military people figured out that they were used to collect weather information and then radio it out for the benefit of U-boats that would have been sneaking down the coast to prepare to attack convoys leaving from Halifax."

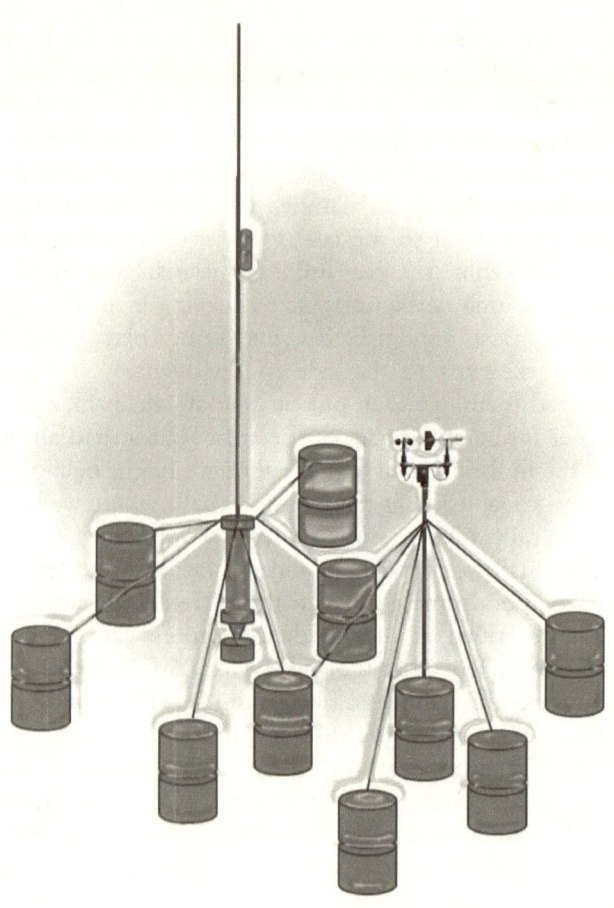

Continuing to step carefully around the site I pointed out the radio antenna attached to the tallest mast and the shorter mast that held the wind vane and anemometer. "I was told that these canisters mostly held batteries to power it all, but one or two of them must have held the measuring parts, a coding machine, and the radio itself," I continued.

At this point, Silver, who had been interestedly sniffing around sounded a low "Yip," to get my attention, and we moved over to see what he'd found. Sure enough, the canister he'd been sniffing at had bright scratches near the latches that held its cover in place.

"Let's not touch it but have a look around and see if any more of these cannisters have scratches on them," I suggested.

The next two cannisters that I inspected just looked rusty and untouched, but a third had scratches, just like the first one.

"Here's another one!" Sharon motioned me over to the canister that stood closest to the one that Silver had found. This one had scratches around its latches too, and it also had a name plate on it that was so weathered, we could barely read it.

"Canadian Meteorological Instruments," Sharon read out, "and some kind of company logo." She sounded disappointed. "Looks like its been a wild goose chase – this is just some kind of old research station."

"Not so fast," I disagreed. "You haven't seen the pictures of the one they found in Labrador but was identical to this one. I think that the name plate is a decoy, put there to avoid suspicion. Let's back up a bit." Saying this, I took a 35 mm camera from my daypack and started taking pictures, up close for the name plate and the various scratches, then from further back to take-in all the various components of the overall system.

"Aren't you going to open them up?" Sharon asked.

"No. I think someone has put the radio transmitter back into use, and not to send weather information out. Let's not give whomever it is any warning just yet. I think we should just leave everything alone and continue our hike as if we'd simply come across an interesting artifact and then moved along."

"If you say so," shrugged Sharon. "Ready to move on then? We can continue south along the ridge and then cut across to the highway and circle back to the truck."

"One last thing," I said and motioned Silver to come with me back to the first canister he'd found for us. Pointing at the scratched latches, I looked into his eyes and said "Scent, Silver. Remember the scent."

As Silver advanced his nose for a serious session of snuffling around the indicated cannister, Sharon chuckled "I thought dog trainers used commands like Sit, Stay, and Heel, but you seem to have your own language."

"You're right, we both had to learn all the standard commands and hand signals during our police dog and handler training, but when it's just the two of us on our own I've been finding that Silver understands a lot more words than he's supposed to, and it means we can communicate much better with each other. In fact, sometimes I find myself using hand signals just to disguise the fact that he understands so much."

"I still think you two make the oddest pair," she said, shaking her head with a grin.

"No argument there," I agreed, and we all set off. The rest of our hike was beautiful but uneventful. I kept my camera out and used it to take some pictures of the stunning coastal vistas that were laid out before us, one to the south and one to the north. Eventually, we turned east into the forest and endured tough going until finally, we emerged at the highway. From there it was an easy walk back to where we'd parked.

"How about stopping for coffee at that last town we came through on the way here," I suggested nonchalantly, I thought, but Sharon wasn't fooled.

"You mean so you can snoop around some more," she accused, smiling.

"Snooping is such a strong word. Let's say taking in the tourist amenities," I countered.

The nearest town was Ingonish, which turned out to be a small village rather than a town. Its main features were an assortment of well-spaced houses, a breakwater protecting a couple of piers to which were tied-up a number of Cape Islander[23] fishing boats, and a quiet, protected beach. It was just large enough, however, to include a small café/gift shop and a full restaurant, both in restored former homes and both with fantastic views of the ocean. We chose the café, partly because it had a couple of tables on a small outside deck and that let us sit and order while Silver lounged on the grass right beside us.

The woman that came to take our order had the traditional Maritimer's ability to spot people who were "from away[24]" and immediately asked me where I was from. "Ottawa, originally, but staying in Halifax for the summer," I replied truthfully, and used the segue to ask her what kinds of things there were to do in the area.

"Hiking, golfing, whale-watching, swimming, lying in the sun on the beach," rolled smoothly off her tongue as if she'd repeated this list a million times before, which I supposed that she had. "The restaurant down the lane is good if you're staying for dinner, but shopping is limited to our gift shop next door and an antique shop that you'll see at the edge of the village on your way back to Halifax.

There were other tourists seated at a nearby table, so we avoided talking about the weather station and simply enjoyed the location and each other's company. Our waitress was kind enough to spontaneously appear with a bowl of water and a soup bone for Silver, who very contentedly laid in the grass working away at the large bone.

There was one other interesting thing about Ingonish, and I almost missed it.

We still had some time before dinner, and Sharon was telling me a story about something or other as we drove through the village on our way to do some more sightseeing. We were just about to turn onto the highway when I suddenly hit the brakes. "Do you mind if we stop in that antique store that we just passed?" I asked.

"Sure, I mean no, I don't mind, why?"

"Just a feeling. I'm curious about it. Besides, it might have some interesting things to see."

"OK, but beware, shops around here price things high for the American tourists. You can get better deals in Halifax," she warned.

"Right," I said, slowly. "I hadn't thought of that. OK, if I get starry-eyed about something, then drag me out of there, OK?"

"Deal," she said.

Turning around, we drove back to the antique store that we'd just passed, Oceanside Antiques, and parked in front. Leaving Silver in the truck, we got out and strolled in.

The store was amazing. It had everything from oil lamps, to furniture, to pictures and books. As we looked around, I noticed that there were a large number of old radios and TVs near the back of the store, all of them in handsome, heavy-looking wooden cabinets.

"Are you interested in vintage radios?" a voice asked.

Startled, I turned to see that a thin, elderly man had quietly appeared at my side.

"I'm not sure," I said, honestly. "I was just thinking that the cabinets made the radios look more like pieces of fine furniture, and how heavy they must be."

"When radio shows became popular, these were intended to be shown off as pieces of fine furniture," the man said. "See how the really old sets, the ones from the 1930s I mean, are just machines, with their tubes sticking up into the air. But in the 1940s and '50s, all across America, and Canada too, families would gather around their radio in the evenings and listen to the news and the popular radio shows. 'Soap Operas' they were called, because the early radio dramas and comedy shows were often sponsored by companies that made soap, and you had to listen to their soap commercials if you wanted to hear the shows." He paused, lost in thought, or more likely memories I thought. "Anyway," he continued, "in those days the family radio was a prized piece of furniture ... not like today with our plastics and our transistors," he added, dismissively.

"Are they hard to fix? I asked.

"Not really," he said, conspiratorially. "The only thing that ever went wrong with radios of this vintage was the vacuum tubes would either burn out or spring a leak and lose their vacuum. All you have to do is find out which tubes have gone bad and replace them.

"But where do you get the tubes then?" I asked, getting more interested now.

"Mostly by swapping tubes from other sets. As you can see, I have a pretty good supply right here," he said, sweeping his arms to the left and right to emphasize just how many of these old radios he had piled up in his shop. "I have a small radio and TV repair shop in the back of the store, and outside of tourist season that's where most of my business comes from," he explained.

I was getting very interested but didn't want to let it show. To change the topic, I asked the first thing that popped into my head: "Do you have any nautical artifacts?"

"Nautical?" he asked, taken off-guard by the sudden change of topic.

"Sorry, I guess that's a stupid question to ask in an antique store, but we were diving on a couple of shipwrecks last week and it's gotten me interested in things nautical."

"There are no stupid questions," he retorted automatically, "only people that are too stupid to ask questions," but I could see that he was thinking.

"Well, I don't have anything off ships, but diving now... I used to have a replica of an old-style diver's helmet, let's see if we can find it, hmm?" Without waiting for an answer, he shuffled off to another corner of his store and started rummaging around behind a large collection of old table and floor lamps, all of which I thought looked quite hideous. I could see that Sharon did too, as I caught a glimpse of her trying to stifle a laugh.

Thinking it was time to move on I had started to move away when the old man said "Here we are. I haven't entirely lost my memory yet!" and he gingerly stepped around his various tables and lamps carrying, as advertised, a replica of an old diver's helmet. Except that it wasn't a life-size replica, it was more like a model. Whereas a real diving helmet is huge and weighs nearly sixty pounds, this one was only about eight inches high and only weighed about two pounds. It was beautiful though! Made of copper and brass, it still had an upper helmet attached to a corselet piece that would sit on a diver's shoulders. The upper helmet had the three porthole-style windows, and the handle on top, to which the tether from the surface would be attached.

"How much is it?" I asked, almost involuntarily.

"Sixty-five dollars," he replied.

"Hmm, that's a bit much for me right now." As I hesitated, Sharon jumped in and said that we'd better get going since we had to make our own dinner yet.

I told the old man that I'd think about it and that we'd probably be back the next week to do some diving for our university projects, so I would come back and see him again.

"Any time," he said. He was used to this.

Driving back to the cottage, I thanked Sharon for providing an excuse for us to leave.

"Were you really so interested in old radios?" she asked. You seemed very focused and then suddenly changed the subject and sent him off to find that model diving helmet.

"Radio receivers, no, but I'm very interested in radio transmitters."

"Transmitters!"

"Exactly, transmitters. That guy must have thought we were just a couple of stupid females, but you have to know more than how to swap vacuum tubes to be able to repair radios and TVs," I said, rather hotly. "Anyway, if he knows how to repair radios, maybe he knows how to fix and use transmitters too."

"Wow, so he's a suspect?"

"I don't know," I said, mulling it over in my mind. "Let's just say that I'm interested in the coincidence of finding someone knowledgeable about old radios that lives so close to a reactivated old radio transmitter."

"And the diving helmet?"

"Now that, I am interested in! I really do want to buy that helmet, but I don't want him to think that I can afford it on a student's stipend. What's more, I really wanted to have an excuse to go back to that shop again, and now we have one."

"We?"

"Well, you still have a Cape Breton dive to do and I may as well do one more as well, so that gives us a couple of excuses to come back up here again."

"Sounds great," Sharon sat back contentedly, and we both enjoyed a quiet drive back to Halifax. I thought that we'd be safe for at least one more trip to the Inverness area and that after that I'd have to take care not to get her involved any deeper.

We drove back to Halifax, and then it took a couple of days to get my pictures developed. I'd ordered two sets of prints, so I could send one set along with the original negatives to Bob in Ottawa and keep the other set for myself. I also wrote out an account of what I'd learned so far, which wasn't much, but I did include the company name from the weather station and asking him to find out anything he could. I sent everything off to him by airmail.

Meanwhile, I tried to do a little digging of my own via the university and city libraries too. I couldn't find any record of a company called Canadian Meteorological Instruments Ltd.

Other than my library research, I spent the rest of the week processing the samples I had collected from our Lunenburg and Polly's Cove dives and getting new sample bottles ready for my upcoming dive in Cape Breton.

It was hard trying to be patient, but by Saturday I was rewarded with a flashing message light on my answering machine. Bob had left a message to call him at his home in Ottawa. When I called him back, he had mixed news.

"There's no trace of a company called Canadian Meteorological Instruments Ltd.," he began.

"So, it's pretty obscure?"

"No, I mean no such company has ever existed in Canada. We even did a trademark search of the logo design you sent the picture of, and we even talked to some people at Environment Canada.

Nothing."

"A red herring then," I hissed. "I thought so."

"Yes, the plot thickens," said Bob.

"So, someone's secretly transmitting something from a hidden location, with a low power transmitter, but what?" I wondered out loud.

"That's what we're going to find out next," said Bob. "You keep on with what you're doing, cover story and all, while I see if I can find someone that can help you out on the radio transmitting side. I'll be in touch."

***

Naval Lieutenant Don Harrison

7 A NEW COLLEAGUE

I thought things must be getting serious for Bob to be arranging for extra help, and this was confirmed by the speed with which it came together. It was only two days later that I received a message to call Bob, and when I got hold of him he said he'd arranged a meeting for me with someone from the military that knew a lot about radio transmissions.

We were to meet at a Harvey's™ restaurant in Dartmouth, part of a Canadian fast-food restaurant chain that specialized in charbroiled hamburgers and fresh-cut fries. I loved going to Harvey's and had spent a lot of time at the one near Carleton in my university days. If this character liked Harvey's, maybe working with him wouldn't be too bad, I thought.

Leaving Silver behind in the truck, I went in. I'd been told to walk in at 7 pm, past the rush hour so it should be quiet, to look for a military-looking person, and to ask him for the time of day. The proper response was to give me an absurdly wrong time. The only other thing I'd been told was that if asked, he'd give his first name as Don. It all struck me as a bit elaborate but being a rookie at this cloak and dagger stuff, I tried to take it seriously.

As I walked into the restaurant, it was quiet all right. I think I must have been looking for someone like Humphrey Bogart in the movie *Casablanca*, with a fedora hat and trench-coat with the lapels pulled up. Fortunately for me, there was only one customer in sight, sitting on a booth at the back. He looked like an actor all right, but more like a young version of Rock Hudson than

Humphrey Bogart, and instead of hiding under a hat and trench-coat, he was very conspicuously dressed in a naval officer's uniform and still wearing his peaked cap. This was definitely not what I'd expected, but with no one else in sight, I was pretty sure that I'd found my contact.

Strolling over to him, I said: "Excuse me, but could you tell me the time?"

"Eleven thirty," he replied with a straight face.

"Don?" he nodded.

"Alexandra?" I nodded in turn and said, "Call me Alex."

"Pleased to meet you, Alex," he said, "Naval Lieutenant Donald Harrison at your service, please call me Don." Then he smiled at me for the first time and I suddenly felt ... interested, in this new acquaintance. I've always thought that I'm more interested in substance than appearances, but this dreamy face and the engaging first impression made me wonder whether I was really a lot shallower than I wanted to admit. Trying hard to maintain a professional outward appearance, I put on a polite smile and shook hands.

"Please join me," he offered. "Or would you like to grab something to eat first? I didn't know exactly when you'd arrive, and I was famished, so I've already started," he said, pointing down at the partially eaten burger and fries sitting in front of him.

"I'm starving too," I replied. "Be back in a second."

Moving back to the counter to place my order and wait for it to be prepared gave me a few minutes to get my thoughts and questions straight in my mind (and my emotions under control too, if I'm going to be completely honest here). Then, supplied with my own tray of burger, fries, and a vanilla shake I went back to join Don in the booth.

"Come here often?" I asked, and then suddenly felt awkward, realizing that I'd unintentionally blurted out a cheesy come-on line.

Don smiled again, to show he appreciated the joke, but saved me with a very genuine-sounding response. "Believe it or not," he said, "I actually do come here a lot. This is my favourite restaurant in the whole area." Waving towards his own food, he added: "it's not fancy but I love these burgers and you can't beat the prices."

I was going to like this guy. "Me too," I supplied, "and I have a hard time not overdoing it on their fries too!"

"I'm glad we're off to a good start... Alex." He'd almost but not quite forgotten my name. "I work alone…," there was an awkward pause, "What I mean is, my work is usually pretty solitary, sitting at a desk and doing paper studies. I'm not used to working with a partner."

Brief aside: At this point, my inner voice was saying: *"This fellow looks like a god, sounds like someone with real character, and he's solitary and shy? Why can't I ever meet someone like this when I'm off duty?"*

"No problem," I said, passing his awkwardness off with a wave. "I get it. I often work kind of alone too, except that now I kind of have a dog as a partner."

"A dog?" he asked, raising his eyebrows and looking around.

"He's in my truck, outside. You can meet him later if you want," I made it sound like a question.

"I always wanted to have a dog," Don mused. "Sure, I'd like to meet him. Where'd you find him?"

"Long story. Ask me another time. Is Don your real name?" I countered.

"Look for yourself," he countered, pulling out his wallet and extracting a card, which he passed over to me.

It was a military identification card, with his picture on it, plus a name rank and serial number. "Lieutenant (N) Donald Harrison," I read out loud. "Naval Lieutenant, that's like a Captain in the Army or Air Force, right?" He nodded. "Looks authentic," I added, handing it back.

"Good, since it's not," Don replied in a very low voice, and then, raising his voice back to a normal volume, "Ask me about it another time, but my name really is Don." Once again, he countered any possible offense with a disarming smile and a genuine-sounding tone of voice.

"OK, answer me this then," I said. "Is this your idea of maintaining a low profile?" I asked looking pointedly at the dress uniform he was wearing.

That got another chuckle. "I know what you mean, but actually, it is. I gather you're not from around here?" I shook my head. "Well, around here naval uniforms are so common that no one gives me a second look. Anyone walking in on us right now would simply assume that it's Friday night, probably date night, and that I just got off work and have popped in to have a quick dinner in the company of a pretty girl. Besides, who's going to be interested in a junior officer? Junior officers like me are a dime-a-dozen around here!"

Ignoring the 'pretty girl' remark, I was trying to come up with a snappy reply when the restaurant door opened, and four people came in. Two guys and two girls, and obviously university students given the textbooks and binders of notes they were all carrying. They dumped the books onto a table and lined-up to place their orders, talking about profs and unfair deadlines, and none of them giving us more than the barest of uninterested glances.

"See?" Don said with a smile.

"OK, fine," I relented, "so where do we go from here?"

"You tell me," Don countered. He was quick though. Before I could retort he'd seen me start to bristle and quickly continued: "Look, all I know is that I was ordered to meet you, find out what I could from you about these mysterious radio signals, and then go out myself with a receiver and try to intercept some more of them."

"How are you going to do that? It'll take forever! And why?"

"Well, first of all, I need to find out where this transmitter is that you've found. Then, I need to find a place where I can work without raising suspicions because I'll have a radio scanner and a recorder. Then, I need to sit tight and listen-in for more signals. If I can record a bunch of signals, then our cryptology people can try to figure out what kind of code is being used, break the code, and then maybe we'll have a better idea of what's going on," he finished, as if it was the most logical and natural thing to be doing.

"But that could take forever," I said, as I tried to picture it in my mind. "What if the signals only go out once in a week, or a month, or several months?"

"I don't know," Don replied frankly, showing some worry for the first time, "but I have my orders, so I guess I'll have to give it a try and see what happens."

"Wow," I gave a low whistle. "I think I'd rather have my job than yours. Is your work always like this?"

"Tedious? Working in the dark, only knowing a little bit about what's really going on?" he asked. "I suppose so," he replied, thoughtfully. "I started out as a CELE[25] Officer in the air force, so I know something about radios. But nowadays, ..." he drifted off, thinking. "You know what branch of the service I'm really in?"

"I wasn't told, but all of sudden I think I do," I nodded.

"There you go then," he nodded in reply. "It's like being a fire fighter or a police officer," he said, looking at me meaningfully. "They spend a lot of time sitting around or doing boring, repetitive work, and then all of a sudden all hell breaks loose and sometimes a lifetime's worth of action and experiences get packed into a few days or weeks."

"Now your job sounds exactly like mine," I exclaimed. Impulsively I reached over the table, offering to shake his hand again. "I'm glad to meet you Don, or whatever your name really is, I think we're going to get along just fine."

For a while, I brought him up to date on how I'd come into the case and what little I knew so far. Since Bob had essentially vouched for him, I didn't hold back and basically told everything. For his part, Don showed himself to be intelligent, a good listener, and able to interject good questions.

"You said that you were in communications engineering?" I'd asked.

"Originally, yes."

"Can you tell me more about this automatic telex business then?"

"You know about telegraphs and Morse code, right?"

I nodded.

"OK, well then, telegraphy didn't completely go away when radio came in," Don explained. "Teletypewriters were invented to eliminate the need for operators trained in the use of Morse code. That automated the message encoding, and they used pulse-code dialing to send telex messages over phone lines and *voilá*, "telex." A similar thing was done for radio. Telex systems were adapted to short-wave radio by sending tones over a single sideband. It's called telex-on-radio, or TOR. It's not very common in North America, but it's still being used in some third-world countries because it's cheap and reliable."

"What's it used for?" I asked.

"One use is to broadcast short weather or news updates. You've heard of organizations like Associated Press and Reuters?"

"Sure."

"Well, at one time that's how news flashes were sent out around the country. The signals would be received on simple, receive-only teleprinters - with no keyboards or dials or anything - and when the teleprinters started hammering away printing something, people would know that there was a news flash and come and tear off the printed paper to see what it was."

"So then, if people thought it was newsworthy they'd print it in a newspaper or read it out over the radio news," I said, catching on.

"Exactly," Don said. "Sending telegrams works the same way, except that there are sending and receiving machines on each end, and message switching systems to route the messages to their target destinations. That's how Western Union works."

"Can it be done in any language?"

"As long as the sending and receiving machines use the same characters. Most teleprinters use English and some special keys, like to signal the beginning and end of messages, and for starting new lines and paragraphs. There even special keys for weather symbols. All of the characters get coded on a simple DC (that's direct current) circuit and sent by turning the current on and off. It's just like the dialing clicks you hear on a rotary telephone. Telex is the same thing but with a lot more characters to send. Big companies like Western Union have computers now, which lets them use fancier coding and faster speeds, but it still comes down to little on/off electrical pulses."

"OK, so then how would you automate the message sending from our mystery station – its small and pretty remote."

"Ah hah!" he responded. "Even in big offices, the teleprinter circuit is usually linked to a 5-bit paper-tape punch and reader, allowing messages to be received and then stored or even resent, on another circuit."

"So," I mused. "If you had the right equipment you could type out a message on one of these paper tapes, at home, say. Then, you could carry the paper tape to another location and read the message in through a paper tape reader, which could then send the coded message out by radio. Right?"

"Right. The military still has systems like that for sending messages out to ships, and bombers, and so on. A really important message might have a special code on it that means Flash-Priority to indicate that the message needs to be read and delivered to the Captain right away."

When we'd gone through everything and finished our dinners, Don thought for another moment, and then said, "OK, I think I've got it. I already had the frequency and now you've given me the location of the transmitter. Give me some time to scout the place and get set up, and then I'll call you to set up another meeting ... it will take about a week. Here's my number at work, it has an answering machine in case you want to leave me a message," he said, writing a phone number on the back of his dinner receipt.

"OK," I agreed and did the same for him. "The lab I'm working out of at Dal is too public, so this is my number at home. I have an answering machine too, so my boss can leave me messages."

"I don't think I've ever met a girl and gotten her number so quickly," he smiled again. Where in the world had he acquired such an attentive manner and such a disarming smile, I wondered?

"Don't get carried away in your role," I warned, archly, but he could tell that my heart wasn't in it. I was going to have to watch myself with this one.

Surprisingly, I didn't get any help whatsoever from the normally over-protective Silver.

As we walked out of the restaurant together, I indicated my truck and offered to introduce Don to Silver, as promised. Don was clearly impressed by the truck and must have momentarily forgotten about the dog because he walked up close to the driver-side door to peer into the window. I'm not sure what he wanted to see, but what he got was a huge white face showing a lot of big teeth, and a volley of loud barking.

Don started and pushed back so violently that he fell backwards to the ground. He was pretty agile though, and recovered himself quickly, turned to me, and said: "That's a wolf!"

"Not a wolf, an Alaskan Malamute, but I have to admit that he does look the part. The first time we met, he nearly gave me a heart attack too!"

Telling Silver to relax, I opened the front door, gave him a vigourous rub on the head, and said, "Silver, I'd like you to meet Don. We're going to be working together now and then."

Don instinctively offered his right hand to be sniffed, which Silver accepted as an appropriate peace offering and gave him a thorough sniffing. Pulling back a bit, Silver looked Don straight in the eyes with that penetrating gaze he could switch on, then he shifted his gaze and looked pointedly at Don's left hand.

"He's smart," Don commented. "Is it OK if I give him a bit of a burger?"

Surprised at both his foresight and his manners I nodded yes, and Don held out his opened hand to reveal several chunks that had obviously been saved from his burger.

Silver 'wolfed' them down in a flash, and then looked up at me as if to say: "I like him!"

***

8 ANOTHER SUSPECT?

The Monday after the weekend, Sharon, Silver, and I drove back up to Cape Breton again. Our first task was going to be the last of the three dives that we'd planned together for our respective research projects. Assuming, of course, that the sea was calm enough. Naturally, I wanted to take a look at (or, as Sharon phrased it, "snoop around") more of the small villages that populated the Cabot Trail every few miles in the Ingonish area.

We'd booked the same cabin near Ingonish Beach as before and, after checking in, we used the time to drive through all the nearby communities. In the 14-mile drive north from the summit of Cape Smokey to where we'd be diving the next day, there are five small communities. Six if you count the small community at the Keltic Lodge resort. These include Ingonish Ferry, Ingonish Harbour, Ingonish Beach, Ingonish Centre, and Ingonish itself. Some of these have only a scattering of homes and a couple of docks for the local fishing boats, while a couple have one or two small restaurants or cafes, and there was an occasional store or gas station.

Ingonish Centre, for example, had a pizzeria, while Ingonish Beach had a restaurant/bakery and a liquor store. We drove through them all, but I didn't spot much beyond houses and fishing boats. Stopping at the few stores and gas station in the area, we met more of the local people, but none aroused any suspicions on my part, or on Silver's. After making our own dinner again, and going for an evening walk, we made it an early night, so we'd be ready for diving the next day.

Sharon wanted to try diving in the bay off Ingonish, which was just south of Bear Cove and the Red Head cliffs where she'd found the old weather station. A small point of land, appropriately named 'The Point' provided some protection from the open sea, but we knew that we were going to have to watch out for rip tides.

This dive was relatively uneventful, compared with our two previous ones. It was another cloudy, grey day. We were able to park near the shore, which was a blessing as that allowed us to avoid a long hike each way, with all of our gear, and we were away from the tall cliffs that were so beautiful but such hard work to carry our gear down and up.

Leaving Silver to lounge on top of our gear bags, we entered the water and swum out a good distance before switching from snorkels to regulators and diving down to the bottom. When we reached the bottom, we were already at 30 feet of depth, and we were almost immediately greeted by lots of marine life. Sharon wanted to collect her sediment samples from below the thermocline, so we followed the bottom out until it kind of plateaued at 55 feet. There had been a strong current pulling at us initially, but at this depth, the water was very calm and fairly clear, about 30-foot visibility. As a result, we had no trouble getting our water and sediment samples.

With our sample bottles in our mesh carry-bags, we each looked around but there wasn't much more to see, so Sharon signaled that we may as well head back for shore. The current had moved us off our intended course a bit, so it was a new route heading back that brought us over some very rocky areas where we had to be careful not to become tangled up in a couple of lost fishing nets. These did not pose a significant danger, as long as we still had lots of air left plus a way to cut them away if one of us got caught on one. In this case, our air supplies were still in good shape, and it was for situations like this that we carried large diving knives strapped to our legs.

In my Ontario and Quebec freshwater-diving days I used to have visions of getting tangled up in an underwater fishing net or line in such a way that I might not be able to actually reach down for the knife strapped to my calf. So, being the worrier that I am, I had adopted the habit of diving with a second knife attached to either my upper arm or to the hose with my pressure gauge on it.

As a result, I wasn't worried about the nets we encountered, but we avoided contact with them anyway.

Rather than surfacing, we stayed on compressed air and followed the rising bottom all the way back in to shore, and I was rewarded by finding a bed of Bar Clams[26], tucked in around the base of a sand bar that we later decided would have been just below the low tide level. This enabled me to grab a bunch of clam samples.

Sharon and I each had a steaming mug of my signature tomato soup while we were changing and packing away our gear and our samples but were still left feeling hungry, so we stopped in at the Ingonish Beach restaurant/bakery for coffee and fresh, hot cinnamon buns. Once again, the restaurant had a small deck outside, so Silver could lie on the grass nearby and keep us company.

We were served by a nice, older lady who stopped to chat a bit every time she came to our table. In this way, we discovered that she and her husband owned and managed the restaurant/bakery, with him being the cook and baker and her the front manager and occasional pitch-in waitress, when needed, to help their one full-time waitress.

The more we spoke, the more I became convinced that I was hearing a very slight German accent in her voice. Curiosity aroused, I was wondering about the husband when Sharon mentioned how much she enjoyed the fresh cinnamon buns. When I added my genuine endorsement of Sharon's praises, she said she'd tell her husband and went off to the kitchen.

Sure enough, when we'd gone inside to pay the bill, he came out of the kitchen.

"So, you like my rolls?" he asked.

We did, and we asked where he'd learned to bake so well. He credited his mother for teaching him. Like so many people for whom English is a second language, the more he talked about his parents and his childhood, the more a very slight accent from his native language set in. German, it sounded like.

My mind was alive with possibilities as we began our drive back to Halifax.

"What are you thinking?" Sharon asked.

"That couple we just met, Henry and Anna Miller – I thought that I detected slight German accents from each of them and I was wondering about their names."

"What about them?"

"Well, a lot of immigrants anglicize their names when they move to Canada or the U.S., and I was wondering whether Henry and Anna Miller might have been Heinrich and Johanna Müller, or something like that."

"Isn't that a bit of a stretch? Why suspect them?"

"I'm not sure that I suspect them, exactly, but there were a few too many coincidences there."

"Like their names and accents?"

"Those, yes, but did you notice the large, floor-model antique radio in the corner of the main restaurant? It was actually working; with those big speakers they used to use the sound quality was actually pretty good."

"No, I heard some music but didn't see where it was coming from. I hadn't thought to look. Is that all?"

"Almost. As we were pulling away, did you happen to notice that tall pole standing behind the closest house to the restaurant? I think that was a ham radio operator's antenna."

"My God, I must be blind!"

"Not blind, it's just that I've been looking for things like that every time we've passed through a village. That was the only one that I've seen. I think I'll ask Ottawa to do some digging for us."

"Us! I like that," Sharon said, excitedly.

Damn, damn, damn. "Promise me that you'll back out of this when I ask you, OK? I don't want to expose you to danger."

"You think there'll be danger?" Sharon asked, still excited.

"I hope not, but I'm getting a bad feeling about all this… Promise me?"

"OK, I promise," Sharon said, giving the Girl Guides' salute.

I hoped that she was the type to keep her promises.

The next morning, I called Bob and asked him to please check into the names Henry and Anna Miller, when they'd emigrated to Canada, whether their original names might have been different, whether Henry had a ham radio licence, whether either of them had a criminal record and anything else they could dig up.

Once again, his people were quick. By Thursday I'd received a message to call Bob. I'd been close on the names. Henry and Anna Miller's immigration records showed them to have entered Canada from West Germany, as a married couple, in 1957 - twenty years earlier. Their original names had been Herbert and Angela Müller. Neither had a criminal record, but Henry had a Class A Amateur Radio Operator Certificate and a radio station licence, both issued in 1966.

Now I had a suspect or two in the Millers and some vague suspicions about the owner of the antique store. It felt like progress.

The following day (Friday) we cleaned our gear and worked in the lab with our new samples. Neither Sharon nor I were quite ready for our next dive or dives, and Don was still off somewhere doing something secret, so Silver and I simply took the weekend off and enjoyed sleeping-in in the mornings and going for long walks. Our new favourite was walking along the many pathways in Point Pleasant Park, which lies at the mouth of Halifax Harbour. Many of the paths eventually led to the harbour-front, with great views, a couple of beaches (although Silver still refused to put more than a paw in the seawater), and a few historical monuments – like the huge anchor from the HMCS Bonaventure, Canada's last aircraft carrier, which had been decommissioned in 1970.

Fortified by our weekend off, it felt like good timing when Sharon showed me the Fisheries Notice on Monday morning. I was in the lab finishing my work with the samples from my last dive when Sharon rushed in excitedly waving a fisheries department notice at me.

"Read," was all she said.

Red Tide Prompts Shellfish Closures

News Release

DARTMOUTH, N.S. – The Department of Fisheries and Oceans (DFO) is advising the public that the levels of paralytic shellfish poisoning toxin (PSP or red tide) are high in numerous locations throughout the coast. Many areas are now closed to harvesting bivalve shellfish due to unacceptable PSP levels. Coordinates of the latest closed areas are outlined below.

Shellfish closures can change frequently, therefore harvesters also are encouraged to call local DFO offices for information on current PSP closures prior to fishing.

- 30 -

I'd been wondering what I'd do next but now, as luck would have it, we had an actual Red Tide alert out. Although she now knew that my research project wasn't strictly real, Sharon thought I would want to head out the next day and get some samples while the Red Tide levels were high.

With nothing better to do, I agreed. Looking at the list of affected areas, I saw that one of them was the entire Ingonish area. It seemed like a sign, so I jumped at the chance to get some Red Tide samples and, more importantly, do a bit more snooping around in Cape Breton. With three sample-collecting dives behind us, we had a system now, so it didn't take us long to prepare. I was looking forward to the dive with Sharon, knowing that it might be my last. With samples collected before and during the Red Tide, there would be no excuse for me to go back again, and no real motivation to collect more samples further south.

That night, I found a message from Jack McDonald waiting on my answering machine. Jack and I had been recruits together at the RCMP Depot Division training centre in Regina, Saskatchewan, and then our paths had crossed again the previous year, when I was on an undercover assignment in Fort McMurray, Alberta. We'd worked well together, and I'd learned that I could trust him. The phone number he'd left had a Nova Scotia area code, and when I returned his call he explained that he was on a temporary assignment to the Baddeck Detachment, where he was filling-in for a constable that was sick and not expected back to work for a couple of months. Apparently, Jack had only just arrived the day before.

I told him that his timing was great because I was going to be driving to Cape Breton the next day and that although I'd be going up with a friend, she knew about my real job and we'd be able to talk reasonably freely.

I thought I knew the answer, but I did ask Jack how it was that he knew where I was and how to reach me.

"Staff Sergeant Simpson called me and asked me to call you," Jack replied. "He seemed to feel that since we'd be in the same neighborhood for a while, we might enjoy a chance to get together over coffee."

"Mmmm hmmm... more like he's found some way to engineer your temporary transfer out here in case I need your help, like I did in Alberta last year."

"All he said was that you were on another undercover mission, and since I'd be coming out here anyway, he thought it would be good for you to have someone nearby that you could call if needed. Someone that would understand what you're doing and not waste time with a lot of damn-fool questions."

"That sounds like a direct quote."

"It is. He didn't give me any details about the operation, but you know you can count on me."

"I do Jack, thank you. By the way, I'm not mad at my boss, things are starting to heat up a bit out here and I might very well need your help before long. I just don't want you getting involved without knowing what you might be getting yourself into."

For the next few minutes I summarized what I'd been sent out to do and the progress I'd made to date. To his credit, none of this fazed Jack in the least.

"Look, Alex, I'm not one for undercover work, much less all this cloak-and-dagger stuff, so I'm happy to leave that to you. But with all your focus on this part of the province, I don't have any doubts about your boss having found some sneaky way to get me transferred out here. As I said, you can count on me."

I sighed. "Thanks, Jack, I really appreciate this."

It was arranged that Jack and I, and Sharon, would meet at a coffee shop in Baddeck the next day before Sharon and I continued to Ingonish.

The coffee shop Jack had recommended was on Water Street, giving us a great view of the inland sea[27] called Bras d'Or Lake. I introduced Sharon to Jack, who'd had the presence of mind to come in plain clothes. Having spent time together the previous year, Silver and Jack recognized each other immediately. Once again, we were able to sit outside so Silver could keep us company, and our server was nice enough to bring out a bowl of water for him.

"He looks like a wolf," she said, as she cautiously set the bowl on the ground a few feet from him.

To this, Silver immediately smiled up at her, with his tongue lolling out.

"It's like he heard me!" she exclaimed.

"I think he really appreciates getting the water. Thank you," I said, to change the topic.

With introductions made and drinks acquired, and with no one else within earshot, I sketched-in the details of Sharon's discovery and my investigation to date. I mentioned that someone from military intelligence was also involved but didn't identify him or provide any details of what he was up to.

Before parting, Jack and I exchanged our home and office telephone numbers, and I told him that I also had a police radio. Following my first undercover assignment in Alberta, a year earlier, I'd asked to have a radio installed in my truck. What I'd wanted was one that looked like a CB radio[28] but that actually worked on the police band. The radio technician that installed it for me had done me one better. The radio inside the cab and the antennas that were conspicuously attached to my oversized rear-view mirrors on each of the front doors not only looked like a CB radio system but if anyone were to turn the system on they would find that it worked like any other CB radio. Almost, that is. The radio technician had explained that he'd tuned the antennas to optimize sending and receiving on the police band, so the signal strength on the CB frequencies wouldn't be as good as it should be. I thought that was unlikely to be a problem. As far as the police band went, the RCMP has a standard frequency that is used by the dispatchers and highway patrol right across the country, plus several tactical frequencies. A hidden switch on my radio allowed me to access these using the ordinary pre-set buttons on the front panel.

Jack said that he was about to start a shift on highway patrol and would just 'happen' to be in the area where the highway ran from Ingonish through to Ingonish Beach and gave me his car number in case we should need to make contact by radio. We made up a fictitious car number for me to use as well. We also agreed that in future, I would call Jack before going to Cape Breton and again on the way out or failing that when back in Halifax. I have to admit that I felt better knowing I had a local ally.

Between the long drive north and our visit with Jack, it was too late in the day and we were too tired for our dive, so we put that off until the next day. After checking into our rented cabin at Ingonish Beach, we had time to spare before dinner and went back to the Oceanside Antiques store in Ingonish. Nosing around the store, I was still fascinated by the old tube-style radios. The man I'd met on our previous visit wasn't there this time, and an elderly lady introduced herself as his wife, Wilma.

Wilma had noticed me looking at a table model radio in a

handsome wooden cabinet and had come over to talk to me about it.

"Are you interested in old radios?"

"Well, I didn't think so, but when I visited your store a few weeks ago I noticed these beautiful old radios, and your husband had explained a bit about them to me. I guess I still find them fascinating. Why do they seem to have so many frequency bands on them?" I asked pointing to the radio I'd been looking at, which had four frequency bands on its main dial.

"This one is a 1947 RCA Victor model," she explained. "In those days people were used to listening to the AM band for music stations, and the short-wave bands for news reports and this radio had the new frequency modulation band, what we now call FM, and which was brand new at the time. The AM and FM bands were popular for local music radio stations, and the short-wave bands were popular for getting new reports from far away stations in the US and Europe. You can see that this model also had the special 'Magic Eye' feature, which was a vacuum tube that you would look at to help get the stations tuned just right. It had a dark centre that would shrink from a circle to a narrow band when a station was properly tuned. The changing shape reminded people of a cat's eye, which is where the name came from."

"Was it that difficult to tune then?" I asked.

"Not for the AM or FM stations, but the signals were much weaker for short-wave stations that were far away, like on the continent in Europe, so the Magic Eye tube really made a difference. Come, let me show you," and with that, she led to way to the back of the store where they had a similar old, multi-band radio that was plugged in. Turning it on she waited a minute for the tubes to warm up and then began turning the tuning dial.

Sure enough, as she slowly moved the tuning indicator we could begin to hear a station come in. The sound was fuzzy at first, then it became clear that someone was talking, and then when the Magic Eye displayed its narrow cats-eye image the voice became clear – it was a man reading a news report.

"There, you see? That's probably a radio station in England or Western Europe transmitting on short wave."

Another working short-wave radio…, I thought to myself. *Oh no.*

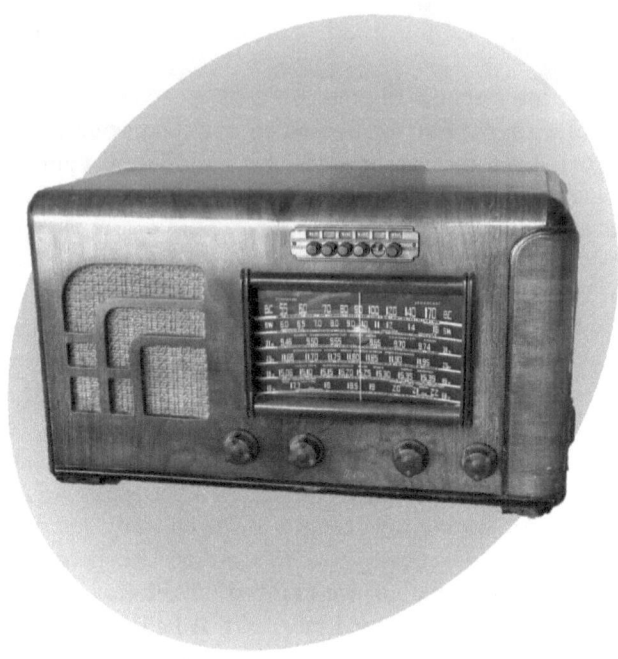

To cover my racing thoughts, I tried to show a polite interest and then change the conversation. The only idea that popped into my head was the model diving helmet I'd seen on my previous visit, so I asked whether they still had it in the store. It turned out that they did, so I looked it over again and decided to buy it. This provided the distraction that I needed and covered my exit from the store. As a bonus, I really had wanted to buy the model helmet so it all worked out well.

As Sharon and I drove to a restaurant for dinner I resolved to send a new message to Bob in Ottawa, asking him for more information on the owners of Oceanside Antiques. Over the previous six weeks, I'd driven and/or walked through every village in the Ingonish area and had looked inside every one of their stores and restaurants. Everything had seemed peaceful and innocent-looking except for the two places in Ingonish that had made my danger-sense tingle.

The next day we did our Red Tide sampling dive at the same location as our previous dive near Ingonish Beach. The main difference this time was that a pretty violent storm had just passed through the area. Its aftermath was a mixed blessing for us. On one hand, the ocean was very calm, so it was easy to get into the water, swim out, and do our dive. On the other hand, the storm had stirred the sediment up so much that visibility was very poor. In fact, in order to make sure we didn't get separated we'd had to use a short piece of rope, about ten feet in length, that had a loop to go over one wrist at each end. This reminded me of my student-era's diving days, in which we'd had to do this in some lakes and rivers, but it was the first time I'd had to do this in an ocean. Despite the visibility issues, we eventually got to the location we wanted and collected the samples we'd needed. It all just took a lot more time and energy than it otherwise would have.

When we emerged from the water, tired but content, Silver was happy to see us, as always, and we took some time to play with him and enjoy the beautiful location. As we packed away our gear and loaded everything into my truck, I reflected that I now had my Red Tide samples, so the minimum results needed to lend credence to my cover story were in good shape regardless of whether I did any more dives or not. That was not only convenient but, as we made the long drive home to Halifax, I reflected that I'd genuinely enjoyed Sharon's company and each of the dives I'd done with her.

Sharon's professional instincts led her to convince me that we should do one more dive, so I could get a second set of 'Red Tide' samples for comparison while the Red Tide notices were still in effect. I didn't really have anything better to do, so the next day we drove south along the coast for what would become our last dive together.

We had a choice of the two previous sites: the one down by Lunenburg, and the one at Polly's Cove, near Peggy's Cove. Although neither of us had fond memories of our previous experience at Polly's Cove, it was a shorter drive so that decided it. I'm glad that we decided to back there because the weather was beautiful, the sea was calm and relatively clear, and we got our samples with no difficulty. Later, at the restaurant at nearby Peggy's Cove, as we sat with Silver in the box of my pickup truck eating seafood chowder and enjoying the views of the famous lighthouse, amazing rocks, and the ocean swell, I felt the most amazing sense of peace and contentment.

When Silver and I got home in Halifax that evening, there was a message from Don on my answering machine, asking me to call him as soon as I could.

***

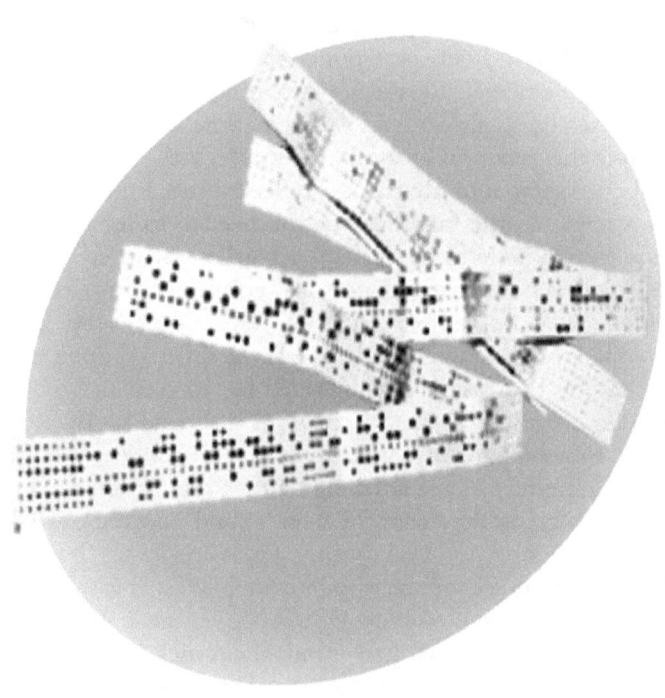

9 DISASTER

When I returned Don's call, I told him about my experiences since our restaurant meeting.

"It feels like I'm making some progress," I summarized, as I wound up my narrative.

"I'm making progress too," he'd said, "do you want to come and see for yourself."

"Sure!"

"OK, how about meeting me tomorrow afternoon at the docks, at Neil's Harbour. That's a small village just north of Ingonish. I have a boat there, and we can cast off at about 4 pm."

I'd readily agreed and the next day Silver and I made the drive back to Cape Breton, and up to Neil's Harbour. All these long drives were making me wish we'd dreamt up a Cape Breton-based cover story.

Parking in a public lot near the docks, Silver and I quickly found Don, who was watching for us. He had rented an older-looking Cape Islander boat.

"The boat is sound," Don said, rather defensively, when he noticed my skeptical gaze scanning the boat. "From the outside, she looks like an ordinary fishing boat, just like the fifty or so others in this area. The owner has been converting her into a touring and diving boat for his own use and started out by completely overhauling all the mechanical systems, so everything inside is in top working condition. The coffee is already on in the galley. Hop in, and we'll get underway."

Silver and I boarded the boat and Don cast off, and expertly navigated his way out of the harbor and south towards the Ingonish area.

"We're heading for Red Head, but not in a direct line. My cover story is that I'm taking hyper-accurate soundings for the Canadian Hydrographic Service. It's nonsense, of course, but it offers an explanation for all the fancy looking electronics that I've had to lug aboard and install. Did you see the long antennas mounted along each side of the boat?"

"Yes, they look a bit like the fishing-net booms that some boats have. The kind that swing out from the sides to support the nets in position when they're fishing."

"Good," Don said with a smile. "That's what they're supposed to look like, or at least to a casual glance. In fact, they are my radio antennas, and they swing up rather than out. You'll see when we get there."

As we continued along, Don explained that he'd been cruising around the area trying to pick-up short-wave radio signals and then triangulating them back to pinpoint their origins.

"How many have you found so far?" I asked.

"Lots of signals of all kinds, of course, but only three that are being transmitted from Nova Scotia. Two of them are ham radio operators."

"Both from people in the Ingonish area?"

"That's right! How did you know?"

I explained about Sharon's and my visit to Ingonish Beach, our meeting with the Millers, and the information I'd received from Ottawa, including Henry Miller's ham radio licence. Clearly, there was a second ham radio operator and I began to wonder whether that might turn out to be Wilma's husband in the antique store, although I'd so far only spotted one tall antenna in the entire area.

"Well, could be, but I have to tell you that so far there's been nothing suspicious about either of their transmissions. One or the other seems to go on the air most evenings after their businesses close, I guess. But when they do, everything is strictly correct. Their transmissions are in plain language, properly identified, and they're pretty typical sounding chatter – mostly with other hams down the coast and in the New England states."

"Rats," I muttered. "That doesn't sound very promising after all."

"Well, the third signal is certainly interesting," Don said proudly. "It's your mystery station!"

"Really? You heard it?"

"Only at first. I was lucky, and just after I got out here it started sending a fairly short message of some kind, in code. It repeated itself every six hours for 24 hours then went silent. There's been nothing in the past week, and I've been snooping around in the area every day!"

"Isn't that a lot of transmitting for our suspect to have do, working from a supposedly secret location?" I asked.

"Not really," Don said. "He only has to go there once, to check that the batteries are OK, then feed in his pre-prepared paper tape loop. Do you remember my explanation of the paper tape recording and re-playing business?" I nodded. "Well, there you are then. They make up the message tape in advance, then feed it in to the machine. The machine is probably preset to transmit the message at intervals for 24 hours and then stop. Our suspect only has to visit the transmitter when there's a new message to be sent, and I somehow doubt that happens very often."

"Simple. Frighteningly simple," I remarked. "How many recordings do you need before the cryptographers can work their magic and decode them?"

"I don't really know," Don replied, thoughtfully. "From what I can understand, it depends on how complex the messages are, whether they repeat enough common words, and so on. I imagine that they are assuming that the language is German, but they would have to bear in mind that it might be some other language, so I don't know what that does to their puzzle-solving. Today, we were lucky again, because when I was out here about three hours ago, it was transmitting again. I only caught the end of the message, but if it repeats itself when we're out there now, we should be able to get the whole thing. That would give us two new messages, plus the first one that started all this."

We were both alone with our thoughts for much of the rest of the trip. It turned out to be the calm before the storm.

As we passed Lakies Head, Don took us out to deeper water but still running parallel to the shore.

It wasn't long before we were passing Broad Cove. As we continued past Red Head and its cliffs, I pointed out the place where we'd found the weather station.

"Should we be hearing something?"

Don laughed. "Not to worry, let's just keep cruising towards Bear Cove." Then, after consulting his logbook, "We're here a bit early. Let's keep going as far as Ingonish Island then circle back and we should be able to catch the repeated message. Then we can call it a day."

As we passed Bear Cove and The Point, I pointed out where Sharon and I had done our most recent SCUBA dive. Don seemed very interested in diving, so this led me to describing some of our earlier dives as well. With stories to tell, the time passed quickly, and soon it was time for Don to take us around the southern shore of Ingonish Island and turn northwest and back to the waters off Red Head. As we did, I mentioned to Don that Ingonish Island looked like a nice place to visit sometime.

Someday, I really should learn to be careful what I wish for.

As we came around the island, Don reduced speed and said, "Here, you take the wheel." As I did, he raised the two big antennas on each side of the boat, switched on his scanning receiver[29], and started his tape recorder running, with its two large reels slowly turning around and around. He had no sooner done this than there was a squawk, and then the sounds of a bunch of pulse tones coming out of the speaker in one of Don's myriad pieces of electronics. Don focused on his equipment, started turning dials and making notes in his logbook, then gave a sharp "Yes!"

Returning to take over the helm, he quickly said, "Let's just troll very slowly around here a bit."

"Is it our mystery station?" I asked, getting excited.

"It sure is, you must be good luck!" Don exclaimed. Within two minutes, the signal abruptly stopped.

"You were saying," I prompted.

"That was it. The messages are only two minutes long, and we just got the latest one!"

Handing me the wheel again, Don went to lower the antennas. He was just in the process of doing this when there was a 'beep' sound from another piece of equipment.

"What's that?" I asked.

"Radar," Don said, turning to look. "It must be a malfunction because it's scanning forward and there's nothing but ocean ahead of us right now."

I could see now that the beep sound had come from a round display screen that had a bright line sweeping around it, like the hour-hand of a clock. As the line swept around, the machine beeped again, and a spot on the screen flared brightly for a moment and then dimmed again.

"Alex," Don said in a measured tone that sounded forced, "Please go back to the stern of the boat, put a life jacket on, grab a second one for Silver, and keep Silver close to you."

Something in his tone commanded instant action, but I did ask "What's going on?" as I passed by him, heading for the stern.

"Something's out there that should not be there, and I think it's heading for us," Don said, "and I have a very bad feeling about it."

"What about you?" I asked, but there was no reply, and I didn't want to distract him.

Reaching the stern, I pulled out two life jackets from one of the storage bins under the aft gunwales. Saying, "Stay with me Silver," I pulled one over my head, put an arm through the armhole of the second, and was trying to find the straps to tie the first one when I heard a loud "Brace yourself!" from Don. Before I could do anything more I felt, and then heard, a heart-stopping crash. Either we had run aground, or something had hit us, I couldn't tell which, and the next thing I remember was the deck being tipped up and me falling backwards into the sea.

Did I mention that the northern Atlantic Ocean is cold? I thought it was bad with a wetsuit to protect me, but with only light clothes and a light pullover on it felt like it must be near freezing. The shock of the cold and the dark of the water completely disoriented me at first, but my instinct to kick for the surface coupled with the lift from the two life jackets soon had my head breaching the surface.

Shaking my head to get the water out of my ears, I looked around. To my left was the shore, I thought. To my right was the boat, but it looked like it had been broken roughly in half, with the broken parts sticking up out of the water and the bow and stern underwater. Calling out Silver's name, I heard a 'yelp' and, turning around, there he was behind me, dog paddling.

So, he could swim after all! That was a relief.

Turning back, I tried to spot Don, but couldn't see anything but the boat. It was surreal, because there was no sound, really. The engine had stopped or been destroyed, there were no explosions, or fires or anything, just a very broken boat that was rapidly settling lower in the water. Then, just ahead and beyond the bow of the boat, I did see something. Something dark – black, or maybe a dark grey in colour – and low in the water. I thought it might be another part of the boat at first, but it was the wrong colour, it was moving away from us, and the shape was wrong.

Taking stock, I tried calling for Don, while struggling to find the straps for my lifejacket and tie them roughly around me. That done, I was able to paddle over to Silver. He seemed OK, but he had a wild look in his eyes that I didn't like. He surely hated being in the water! Eventually, I decided that the best way to help him was by putting the lifejacket under his chest, putting each of his front legs through the armholes of the jacket, and then tying the straps over his back. That way, his chest and abdomen got most of the lift, he could easily keep his head out of the water, his front legs could paddle a bit, and his back legs could still paddle freely.

With one hand on Silver's lifejacket and the other arm stretched out in front of me, I side-stroked as best I could and headed us toward the shore. It seemed to take forever, but eventually my shoulder and hip brushed over some rocks, then the swell pounded us against some other rocks, and I was eventually able to stand up and tow Silver to the shallows. Then, finally, we both kind of crawled up onto the beach.

There was good news and bad news on the beach.

The good news was that we found Don. Not far away from where we'd landed, he was lying in a crumpled heap, exhausted but breathing. He said that he hadn't had time to get a lifejacket, had been partially submersed while still in the boat, and it had taken all his strength to extricate himself from the wreck and swim to shore. With no lifejacket on, his head had been low in the water, so that he hadn't seen me, nor me him.

The bad news was that what I'd taken to be the shore was the shore of Ingonish Island, not the mainland. With hindsight it was obvious, of course. We hadn't had to swim all that far to get to it. As I was considering what to do next, I noticed Don staring out at the ocean – but there was nothing in sight.

"All gone," Don said, softly, between shivers. "So quickly, too."

"What happened?" I asked, and then before he could answer,

"Never mind, we need to warm up first or we'll freeze to death. I think we're on the island, what do you want to do? As I see it, we can try to build a fire here, try walking around to the other side of the island and build one there, or go around and then try to swim for the mainland."

"That's a one-mile swim, and it's a half-mile to get around the island according to the chart. If you'll excuse me not being very macho right now," he said, between shivers, "I vote for building a fire right here on the island, but on the other side. That way we'll be sheltered from the worst of the wind."

So that's what we did. Fortunately, none of us were actually injured in the wreck. We were just exhausted and cold. The short hike got the blood flowing well enough, but with soaked clothing, it didn't seem to warm me up at all. One blessing was that we found a fire pit on the other side of the island. It even had a large pile of wood to one side, that had been split and covered with a tarp to keep most of the wood more-or-less dry.

"This must be a picnic site for boaters in the area," Don said, looking it over in approval. But we still need a way to make a fire and I don't have any matches on me. How are you at rubbing sticks together?" he asked me, trying to lighten the mood.

"Terrible! But if we can find some dry kindling, I might have a trick left up my sleeve," I replied.

He raised an eyebrow at this but didn't comment further and set about looking for dry kindling. There wasn't much to be found.

"You know, in Girl Guides, we were taught that dead branches that are still attached to their trees stay dry and make good kindling," I said as I reflected on moments from my youth.

"That we have," said Don, briskly, and the two of us set about stripping all the nearby trees of their dead branches. These were actually quite plentiful and in a wide range of sizes so that we soon had two large piles of dry kindling, roughly sorted by size.

"I guess the people around here don't know that trick," said Don, appreciatively. "OK, Miss Magician, what's your idea for starting the fire?"

"Don't get the wrong idea now," I said, and proceeded to pull off my wet pants.

"I'm all eyes!"

"I can see that," I said, dryly, "It's your thoughts I'm worried about."

If Don was about to continue the banter, he was cut short by the sight of the bandage on my leg. "You're hurt," he exclaimed, the concern plain in his voice.

"Not hurt. Watch," I said and, gritting my teeth, I ripped-off the bandage that had been concealing my UDT knife. Then, having built a small pile of the smallest bits of kindling wood, I used the knife to add a cluster of shavings from some of the larger kindling, then twisted the end cap to release it.

"A fire starter," Don whistled. Actually, he was shivering too hard to whistle, so it came out more like a wheeze, but I knew what he meant.

"It's called ferrocerium," I said, repeating what Scotty had told me so long ago (*was it only a month ago?* I thought). "It's a metal alloy that you're supposed to be able to strike with a knife blade to create extremely hot sparks. I haven't had a chance to try it before, but this seems like the time."

As Don watched, fascinated, I used the knife blade to carefully scrape some shavings of metal onto the top of my little tinder pile, and then reversed the blade and tried striking it against the ferrocerium rod with a downward, glancing motion. I was rewarded with a few small sparks that were quickly extinguished. I sighed.

"Don't give up now Alex, you've got this," encouraged Don.

I tried again, this time with much more force, and was rewarded with several small showers of sparks that eventually ignited some of the metal shavings. Those shavings burned hot, as the exposed pieces of metal oxidized vigorously in the air. At this, I set the knife down and started to gently blow on the glowing strips of metal as, one by one, they ignited and began to glow white hot. Their heat gradually produced a few slender streamers of smoke from the wood kindling, and with constant, careful blowing I could eventually see some reddish glow coming from the wood itself.

It got easier from there. As the wood began to catch I carefully added some more small twigs and branches, and then built a teepee of medium-sized pieces over top.

"Girl Guides again?" asked Don, admiring my little teepee of firewood.

"Yes, this part I've done before. Once the fire picks up a bit more we can start adding the larger branches, and when we have a solid bed of coals we can start putting the split logs on."

After carefully blowing and feeding the fledgling fire some more, I eventually decided it wasn't going to go out on me and stood up. It was a relief to be able to catch my breath and stretch my back, but I was shivering pretty strongly now. We were going to need heat, and soon.

Fortunately, Don was starting to feel better, despite his shivering, which hadn't relented since we'd met on the beach in the first place. With a brusque "My turn to help," he rose and went over to the tarp-covered pile of split wood. Removing the tarp, he started taking the wood pile apart and moving the split firewood closer to us and then began to construct a wall with it.

As he built it up, layer by layer, I asked "A wall?"

"A wall," he confirmed. There's enough wood here to make a very nice wind-break, and once the fire builds up it will reflect some of the heat back to us if we sit right in front of it.

"I don't think I would have ever thought of that," I commended him.

"Well, fair's fair. You got the fire going in the first place," he said, helping me to put some larger pieces of wood on the fire, which was really taking hold now. We could finally feel some warmth from it seeping into our hands as we fed it with the larger branches.

Once Don had the wall built up about three feet high, he decided that was enough for now and retrieved the tarp, which he shook out and then laid over the wall so part of it hung from the top of the wall down to the ground, and then about three feet towards the fire. Underneath the horizontal part, he placed the two lifejackets I had brought with me. They were soaking wet, but the tarp kept the water away from us.

"Seating for two!" he said with a flourish, and when I moved over to sit, he busied himself with putting the first of the large pieces of split wood onto the collapsed, burning remnants of my firewood teepee, saying over his shoulder "I think you should get out of the rest of those wet clothes."

He was right, of course, so I peeled off my wet clothes and sat huddled in front of the growing fire, feeling warmth starting to enter the rest of my body. "At last," I sighed.

Don stripped off his wet clothes too, but not before making another pile of wood near the side of the fire over which he draped my wet clothes to dry. He made another makeshift drying rack for himself on the other side of the fire, and his clothes soon followed.

Sitting side by side, but not touching, we could both feel the warmth from the fire seep into our bodies, and we were each able to wrap a bit of the tarp around our outward-facing shoulders, which cut more of the wind off.

Then, glancing over at me for the first time since unclothing, his face immediately went back to concern again.

"Is that other bandage a knife too, or are you really are injured after all?' he asked.

"I'm fine now that this fire's going," I assured him. "There's a Derringer under that other bandage."

"Really?" Don exclaimed, amazed again. "You're serious, aren't you?"

"I'll show it to you if you keep on staring at me like that," I said, without a smile, but just barely. He knew I was joking.

"Another time then," Don laughed. "Your first miracle is more than enough for me, for one night anyway."

Then, before the conversation could get awkward, we were interrupted by Silver who had long since shaken the excess water out of his fur, and who had been sitting close to the fire from the moment it had taken hold. Now, however, he had decided it was time to make himself a bit more comfortable, and he weaseled and squeezed his way in between Don and I and settled down in the warmest spot in the whole site, with the windbreak behind him, the fire in front, and two human bodies radiating warmth from either side.

"He's either chaperoning us, or he's the smartest one here," Don chuckled.

"Probably both," I agreed.

With our survival assured, for the moment, we finally had a chance to discuss our adventure.

"Something hit us!" I exclaimed, "and afterward I thought I saw something moving away from us, low in the water."

"Right on both counts," agreed Don, morosely. "I'm sorry, Alex, but I truly did not see that coming or I'd never have asked you to come along with me today."

"What was it? At first, I thought it must be a whale or something, but it didn't look round, it looked angular."

"Mmmm hmmmm, and a whale would have given us a shock, but it wouldn't have sunk us... I think it was a sub."

"What? No! Things like that don't happen anymore," I asserted. Don was silent, letting the thought sink in.

"Right?" I asked, less certain now.

"I'm afraid we made somebody feel very worried. Worried enough to take the risk of sinking us and possibly getting spotted. That means this is no small thing that we're prying into Alex."

"So, the sub was here to receive the coded message," I said out loud, thinking it through. "That's why the message gets sent out repeatedly over a 24-hour period because they can't predict exactly when the sub will be waiting offshore."

I started ticking things off then, lining them up in my mind. "Low power, coded messages are being sent out to where a ship or a submarine can receive them. It's about something important, something secret, but the messages are brief. At least so far, right?"

"Right," Don agreed. "I think you're on the right track, but my guess is that the messages are simply providing dates and times and places for people to meet to exchange something bigger."

"And it's probably whoever is on land that is setting those dates, times, and places. If it was a ship or sub they could just transmit them and the person on shore could listen in on any short-wave radio set."

"That would be my guess," agreed Don.

"But who?"

"Who?" Don echoed.

"Whose sub was that?"

"Ah. Well, it's the cold war, right? My guess would be East Germany, the Soviet Union, or another of the Soviet satellite countries. It doesn't matter, really. It all comes to the same thing."

"So, it's espionage after all," I mused. I explained to Don that we had considered that the messages might have had to do with organized crime in some way.

"Seems unlikely, now."

"What do you think will happen next?"

"Well, I imagine that our masters will ask us to keep digging. No one is going to declare war over the mystery sinking of a fishing boat. We don't know whom to accuse, and even if we did, they'd deny it, claim the boat sank for some other reason, and that if we think we saw a sub we must have been drunk or delusional. Who would contradict them? … Besides us, of course."

"Damn and damn," I cursed.

"Yeah," was all Don said.

"If we're right, then they won, didn't they? They sunk us to prevent you from intercepting their message. All three of us came up to the surface between our boat and the island, so they may not have seen us in the water, but they didn't even bother to check to see if anyone survived. Did they? That must mean that they didn't care, as long as the message remained secret."

"I'm afraid so. On the other hand, if they thought we had the message, and if they knew or suspected that we have more of their messages, then they'd be worried about us breaking the code and breaking up their meetings, whatever they are. In that case, they'd probably just shift their operations to another place, maybe use other methods, and other people. Their agent here could just retreat back into hiding for a while, or forever if necessary."

"But how does that help us?" I asked. "They're probably thinking that they're safe for the moment, but we don't have any of your tapes." Then I looked at him more closely. "We don't have the tapes... do we?"

"Well, I wouldn't say that..." In the fire light, I could see that Don's eyes were twinkling now. Then he reached over to his bundle of wet clothes, rummaged around a bit, and produced a cloth bag with long straps dangling from it. "This is the reason you didn't see me for a while when the boat was hit. I grabbed my earlier tapes, ripped the new one off the front of the recorder, stuffed them all into this bag and tied the drawstrings around my waist."

"Are you crazy? You're lucky you didn't get trapped and go down with the boat!"

"Well, actually, I did. By the time I had the bag tied around my waist, the bow section was almost completely under water. Since it was settling slowly, I decided to wait until the water reached the ceiling, then held my breath for a bit longer. When it felt like my lungs were going to burst, I swam out and up to the surface. When I got there, I used some floating debris to hide behind. I heard you call for me and tried to answer back, but I guess you didn't hear me. From the sound of your voice I judged that you were closer to shore than I was, so instead of using up my strength yelling I decided to follow you in."

"You took an awful chance, Don, but I'm glad you made it. Are the tapes any good now?" I asked, looking at the wet bag dubiously.

"I think so. I'll send them in so someone who knows what they're doing can deal with them, but a short dunk in the water won't erase a magnetic tape. I broke the reel tearing the new one away from the recorder, but they'll be able to wind the tape onto a new reel easily enough."

"So that means we'll have three different recordings all told," I said excitedly. "I hope that's enough to break the code."

"We'll see."

"Seems like I'm not the only magician around here," I said, leaning back against our wooden wall and feeling the heat from the fire course through me. We were each alone with our own thoughts for a moment, and it occurred to me that I had rarely met a man who was so comfortable with silences. I liked it.

We both jumped, then, as a log in the fire suddenly popped and cracked. Don reached over to throw a couple more logs on the fire. Bigger pieces now.

"Don," I said tentatively. Then when he turned to look me in the eyes, "you didn't build this wall just to keep the wind out, did you?"

"No. I'm sorry Alex. I'd hoped you wouldn't notice, but I think it would be safer if no one saw a light coming from this spot tonight. Don't you?"

"I'm glad you're here," I replied. "I don't like this cloak and dagger business. I don't have the mind for it."

"Are you kidding? Look at you. You've survived a shipwreck, looked after Silver there, looked after me, got a fire started when everything's wet and we have no lighter or matches. You know that someone very nasty has just tried to kill us and you're sitting here with me, naked and shivering, but you're holding your own in thinking everything through, and I bet there's more, isn't there?" he challenged.

"What do you mean?" I asked, but I knew what was coming.

"You're not going to give up, are you? No matter what anyone says tomorrow, you're going to keep on until you get to the bottom of this thing, aren't you?"

"I suppose I am…" I said. I hadn't framed it quite so explicitly in my mind as Don had just laid out but, examining my feelings, I found that I couldn't disagree with him either.

"Do me one favour?" he asked. "Let me help…" then he put

his hand out, palm up. "Partners?"

I sighed because he was right again. My first instincts were to try to keep him out of danger, as they would now with Sharon. But, after hesitating a moment, I realized that in his case I was being foolish. Resolved, I put my hand over his, palm down. "Partners," I agreed.

Silver surprised us both then, by standing up and placing one of his forepaws on top of mine, then he raised his head to the sky and let out a defiant howl that would have made his wolf ancestors proud.

"The Three Musketeers, '*All for one, and one for all*,'" quipped Don. "Does he actually understand what we were just talking about?" he asked, in amazement, watching Silver as he sat back down and snuggled up between us.

"I really don't know," I said, thoughtfully. "But, and I know this is crazy, I think he understands exactly. Not the words or the details, but the big picture and the emotions... he always seems to understand the important parts."

"This is a very strange dog."

"You don't know the half of it," I confirmed.

"Rrrrrrrr," growled Silver, low and contented.

***

We didn't talk much after that. There was no need, and we were exhausted. Eventually, our clothes dried out and we were able to get dressed, which added a bit more warmth and comfort. We didn't need to worry about posting a lookout, as Silver would detect an intruder sooner and more reliably than either of us could, but we did resolve to take turns sleeping versus tending to the fire. You'd think we'd have been famished, but I think our adrenaline levels were still up and we were both mostly just sleepy. That would change soon enough.

I was to take the first shift sleeping, and the last things I remember saying to Don before I fell asleep was "What a way to celebrate Canada Day!"[30]

Don, by the way, cheated and let me sleep through the whole night. I awoke with the dawning sun, ravenous but alive!

As it turned out, we were able to attract the attention of an early morning fisherman. Don told him that our boat had struck a shoal and sunk, but otherwise stuck to the truth. The fisherman was sympathetic.

"These kinds of things happen all too often," the man asserted. He kindly agreed to take us all the way back to Neil's Harbour.

It was Saturday morning. Amazingly, we both still had our keys: Don in his pants pocket and me in the jogger's belt-pouch that I had worn instead of taking a purse. Our vehicles were still where we had left them. Although we needed food, I had no intention of letting us be seen in any of the Ingonish area villages, so we drove sixty miles further south, and pulled in at a restaurant in Baddeck.

The nice thing about small towns and villages is that dogs don't have to be tied up or on leashes – at least, not if they are well behaved. I always kept dog food, water, and dishes for them in the truck, so we were able to set Silver up with everything he needed in the box of my truck before Don and I went into the restaurant to eat. The food and surroundings weren't fancy, but I think it was probably the best meal of my life. Silver probably thought so too!

Neither of us had the energy for the long drive back to Halifax so we got rooms at a local motel for the night. Baddeck had a liquor store, so we also made an important stop there. It's not what you're thinking. The fisherman that had so generously taken us all the way back to Neil's Harbour, had absolutely refused to consider taking any kind of payment from us, saying that we'd have done the same for him. That was true but beside the point. We did manage to get his name, at least, and later thought of another, alcohol-based, way to thank him.

Since we were in Baddeck, I gave Jack a call. Jack was staying in dormitory-style accommodation at the local Detachment office, so he didn't have a place, as such, and suggested we meet at a local restaurant for dinner. When we had all converged at the restaurant, I introduced Jack with a few words about our training days and my Alberta adventure. Don introduced himself as a Captain in the Military Police and handed Jack a business card that stated the same. I raised a questioning eyebrow at this change in identification, but all I got I return was a broad, mischievous smile, so I filed my questions away for another time.

Jack was suitably amazed at our story and promised to keep it to himself as I still had to report it all to Ottawa, and we suspected that Bob and his military counterpart would want to keep it all secret. We had a nice dinner together, but Don and I were pretty exhausted, so we made it an early night and headed to our motel rooms for the night. For my part, I called in a lengthy verbal report for Bob in Ottawa. Once I'd contacted his special number I just gave the whole verbal dump – I knew it would all be recorded – and asked the desk officer to make sure it got to Bob the next morning, and then I dropped into bed with Silver curled up beside me and immediately fell asleep.

After sleeping in late the next morning, Don and I met for breakfast, then searched out where our rescuer lived, snuck up, and left a case of rum and a thank you note on his back doorstep. Only then did we each drive our vehicles home to Halifax. As I was driving back, I mentally reviewed everything that had happened to date and then my thoughts turned to Jack and Don. They'd seemed to get along well the previous evening over dinner, but I didn't have a read yet on what they actually thought of each other. I found that I liked them both, but in different ways.

Appearances can be so deceiving, I thought. Jack looked quite plain but was a compulsive Don-Juan-type when it came to women. As early as basic training together, I'd learned that his motto could easily have been "Love 'em and leave 'em," as the old saying went. In other ways, he was fun to be with and our previous experience together in Alberta had demonstrated that I could trust him. Don, on the other hand, looked like a young Rock Hudson, always acted like a perfect gentleman, to use an old-fashioned term, and his strengths seemed to somehow complement mine.

Anyway, once we made it back to Halifax we agreed that we'd each file our proper reports, he'd pass along his magnetic tapes, and that we'd wait for developments. It was a Sunday, so it was decided that in the absence of anything else happening, he'd come over to my place the next evening for dinner.

For my part, I retreated to a long, hot bath accompanied by a restorative glass (OK, two glasses) of brandy. I'd no sooner gotten out of the tub, finally feeling genuinely warm, when Bob phoned from his home in Ottawa.

I'd begun with "Sorry to disturb your Sunday evening," but he quickly brushed that aside and asked what was up. I didn't repeat the details of the report I'd already filed, but I supplemented the things I knew with everything I thought I knew, and some of what I suspected. Bob didn't interrupt a single time, and when I was finished, the line remained silent for a while as he thought it all over. He expressed suitable amazement at my adventure and our narrow escape from drowning, freezing, or starving. I expected that, but his next remark came as a surprise.

"I'll pull you out if you want Alex. I didn't expect things to go this far."

"That's one of the things Don and I talked about over the last couple of days," I replied. "By the way, is his name really Don? He always seems to be pretending to be a different person."

That got a chuckle. "Yes, his name's really Don, but he certainly is more than he seems on the surface. I'm glad he was there with you, and that you looked after each other so well."

"Well, that's a relief. Anyway, Don and I decided we both want to see this thing through. Right about now he's probably having a similar conversation with his boss, although I don't know whether he'll have a choice about staying on."

"He'll have a choice, but he'll stick to this thing like glue. I know Don and his boss, my counterpart, quite well, and they're both solid." In Bob's book, good dependable people were 'solid.'

As he was saying this, I began to think of the whole thing as a chess game, with Bob and his counterpart at Military Intelligence (or wherever) moving their pieces around the board, with Don and I as rooks, sneaking around corners, while supporting and protecting each other, and people like Jack and the cryptographers in important but narrower supporting roles, like pawns in some greater game.

Realizing that Bob had finished speaking, I came alert with a start. "Well, for my part, I want to see this thing through. I think my cover's still intact, although Don's might not be… Anyway, I'd like to stay on."

"Cover not blown? Are you aware how much people talk in those small villages of yours? How many red-headed women with a dog that looks like a wolf do you suppose there are in all of Cape Breton right now?"

"Oh…"

"Yes, 'Oh.' Anyway, you might be right about your cover being intact. Maybe they're only talking about the crazy people that wrecked their fishing boat and had to be rescued." Bob's good humour was back. "In any case, you're no longer inconspicuous, and it's best if we assume that your cover's blown. My advice is to lie low in Halifax for now. If the cryptology people can crack the code and give us a date, time, and place, then maybe we can arrange to eavesdrop on them. We'll have to wait and see. Meanwhile, I'm still working on what I can find out about your antique people."

I'd just like to say right here that I did try to follow his advice.

10 THE GAME IS AFOOT

As planned, Don came over the next day, and since it was only late morning, we decided to take Silver for a walk down to the waterfront. As we walked across the Halifax Commons and past the Citadel, we reviewed everything that had happened over the previous 48 hours. Don agreed that our covers had most likely been exposed and that he too was supposed to 'keep his head down.' While Bob's people were trying to learn more about the Oceanside Antiques people, Don's people had retrieved the messages from his tapes and were trying to figure out how to decode them.

There didn't seem to be much either of us could do for the moment, so we decided to just enjoy our walk and what had developed into quite a nice afternoon. When we reached the waterfront, we turned and followed the docks as closely as we could, walking towards the mouth of the harbor. Being next to the downtown core, there were lots of people out for strolls and just sitting on benches along the way – business people, locals, and tourists alike – all brought out by the nice weather. Well behind us were the navy yards, with a few destroyers tied up, and well ahead of us were the container-ship piers, with their container yards and huge rolling cranes for loading and unloading the containers.

In contrast to the military and commercial sections, most of the boats tied up along these piers comprised pleasure craft, tour boats, and an assortment of tugboats. Most people were looking interestedly at the various boats as they strolled by. I was one of these, so it was while I was eyeing a medium-sized tugboat and wondering whether it could be converted into a floating recreational vehicle of sorts when I realized that someone other than Don was addressing me.

"Excuse me," said a voice, "but aren't you the young lady that bought a model diving helmet from me recently?"

Turning, I saw that it was the couple from the antique store in Ingonish. "Why yes, I am. It's sitting on the mantle in my house right now."

"Well, I'm glad to hear that you're happy with it. My wife tells me that you're interested in old radios too."

"Only because they're so different from what people use now, and I really like the big wooden cabinets and the glow of the tuning band panels."

"You must come to see us again sometime, and I'll show you some more. Do you come to Cape Breton often?"

"I was up several times SCUBA diving with a colleague, but I think it may be a while before we're up again." All my danger senses were screaming at me, but I did my best to keep a straight face and a relaxed tone of voice. I was trying so hard to be nonchalant, that I didn't at first notice what Silver was doing. He had slowly gone up and sniffed all around Wilma, who had nervously backed up a step.

"He won't hurt you," I said, "by sniffing you he's trying to learn about you. Try offering him your hand."

As she slowly held one hand out, Silver sniffed it closely and then gave it a tiny lick with his tongue, which provoked a tiny smile from Wilma.

"Here boy," the man said, holding out his hand to be sniffed.

In this case, though, Silver gave his hand two sniffs and then immediately sat down and stared back at me.

I knew that look! It was time for us to move along.

"Well, it was nice seeing you again," was the best I could manage to say. "I'll drop by the next time I'm in Cape Breton," and with that, I took Don's arm in mine and moved forward to continue our walk, with Silver following close behind.

Don had remained silent and seemed to have barely been noticed during this entire exchange. He was quick to follow my lead though and seemed to enjoy having the two of us walking arm-in-arm. When we were at least a quarter mile further along the docks, I spotted a café with a waterfront deck and suggested we stop there for coffee. We were able to get an outside table on the deck and were the only ones there. With our backs to the café's main window and facing the water I thought it would be safe for us to talk. Since it was so quiet, the waiter said that Silver could stay with us as long as he curled up down around our feet and didn't disturb anyone that might come along.

"What was that all about?" asked Don as soon as the waiter had taken our order and left.

"That was the couple I met at Oceanside Antiques in Ingonish. The man is the one I met the first time I was there, and the woman – Wilma – is his wife. I think that they are the owners of the place."

"OK, so?"

"So, the first time I went up to Cape Breton it was so Sharon could show me where she'd stumbled across the old weather transmitting station. Silver found a couple of cannisters that showed signs of being recently opened and I asked him to remember the scent."

"You asked him to remember the scent," Don said, in a neutral voice.

"Don't look at me like that. I'm not crazy." Don kept looking at me. "OK, well I'm not completely crazy," I modified. That provoked a smile from him.

"Do you remember when I told you that I had a dog as a partner?"

Don nodded. "As a friend too."

"Right, well it's the literal truth in this case. Last year Silver and I were trained to function as a police dog and handler team. When we're tracking a scent, Silver's signal that he's found what we're looking for is to immediately sit at attention and look directly at me."

"I saw that," said Don, getting interested now. "But that was, what, a month ago, can he remember scents that long?"

"It was just over three weeks ago, and I don't know how long he can remember scents, but the one at the weather station is the only one I've asked him to remember while we've been out here, and I know that look that he gave me."

"So, you think he's the one that's maintaining the station and sending the messages?"

Laurie Schramm

"I do. My only real suspects so far have been the couple that run the café/gift shop and these two. All four of them live in Ingonish."

"You think they know who you are?"

"I think so. I think when they spotted me they came up to talk to us purposely, to see if I'd give myself away."

"Do you think they know who I am?" Don asked.

"My guess is that they heard the stories of a man and a woman and a big dog having their boat sunk and being rescued. They probably put two and two together as far as Silver and I but it didn't seem like they paid much attention to you."

"If you're right then they'll now be guessing that it was me with you and Silver on that boat. So... if the sub radioed in that they'd sunk a boat they suspected of monitoring their communications..."

"... and if they felt secure thinking that any recordings had gone down with the boat..." I supplied.

"Then these two would now know that we survived the wreck." Don nodded, thoughtfully.

"Would they suspect that we have the tapes too?" I asked.

"I think so," concluded Don. "These are cautious people that have probably been in this game for a very long time. If so, they've survived without detection by being very careful. If I were them, I would now assume that we have recordings, and I'd assume that we have enough to have broken the code by now too."

"Then if the last message was to set up some kind of meeting they would want to call it off or change it."

"I think so. That's what I would do."

"We have to stop them!"

"Just the two of us?"

"Three of us," I said, looking pointedly at Silver.

"Right," Don said, chuckling. "OK, if we assume that they've headed for home it will still take them awhile to drive, then write and code a new message, print it on tape, and then get the tape over to the transmitting station. That should give us just enough time to call in to our bosses and then hightail it up there."

***

We took a taxi back to my house, to save time, and then took turns calling in to our bosses. It was still early afternoon, Ottawa time, and I was able to reach Bob right away. We each had news.

"First of all, we're going to remain silent about that submarine you encountered. We don't know how much they know about what we know, and they may think that you and Don are dead, so there won't be any news flashes or diplomatic protests."

"We don't really know very much yet, do we? I mean, who would you even protest to?"

"Well, we're making progress on a number of fronts and I suspect that the sub was East German. I thought you and Don might like to know that you've made a little bit of Canadian history. The last time German submarines attacked ships in Canadian waters was off the Newfoundland coast in 1942[31]."

"That's kind of cool, actually. I'll tell Don."

"OK, and we've done some research on Oceanside Antiques. The business is owned and operated by a Marcus and Wilma Light."

"So, the man I met there the first time is probably Marcus Light," I supplied.

"Sounds like it, and Marcus...."

"Has a Ham Radio Licence?" I supplied.

"It's not polite to steal my revelations," admonished Bob, but I could tell from his tone that he was amused rather than upset. "Fine then, you were right, it turns out that Marcus Light has a ham radio licence. Do you want to guess when he first got licensed?"

"Judging by all the old radios and TVs in his shop I'd say the 1960s?" I guessed.

"Earlier than that! He received a Class A Amateur Radio Operator Certificate and a radio station licence in 1947."

"1947! Isn't that about when the Cold War started?"

"Go to the head of the class," Bob said approvingly. "I think you've found our mystery man. We even have his Call Sign, and it matches some of the transmissions that Don intercepted, although I doubt that we'll learn anything useful from transmissions made from his store."

"No, Don said the same thing to me a few days ago."

"I'm trying to get a photograph of Marcus for you, but this is where it gets really interesting because there are some things we haven't found for this Marcus Light: there is no passport, no birth record, and no record of him entering the country."

"Nothing?"

"Nothing. Now that isn't conclusive, because most government departments are still in the middle of computerizing their paper records. It could be that we just haven't found them yet. The records might be missing, or maybe the reason we can't find any birth or entry records is that they don't exist for that name."

"You mean he's a spy?"

"Well, not like James Bond, but yes he could be an agent of some kind. This kind of thing has happened before. Not often, but occasionally[32]. Anyway, we'll keep digging."

"Well, I suspect he has a driver's licence because Don and I just ran into him here in Halifax," I supplied. When I'd related the story of our encounter Bob agreed that we seemed to have found our mystery message transmitter.

"Be careful Alex, they're certainly on to you both now."

"I know, but if Marcus Light is going to try to send a warning message out, Don and I need to get up there right away if we're going to stop it."

"OK then, I'll contact the Baddeck Detachment and get them to have Jack meet you on the way up. If the situation warrants it, he'll be able to call for additional backup."

"Thanks, Bob. I'll call in later tonight whichever way this plays out."

"Good luck."

"Thanks, I hope we won't need it."

Handing the phone over to Don so he could call his boss, I made some coffee to take with us and grabbed a jacket to toss into my truck.

When Don got off the phone, he found me rummaging through a briefcase in the spare bedroom that I'd been using as an office.

"Ready to go?"

"I am now," I answered, showing him my badge and Silver's official police identity card. "Do you still have that military ID of yours?"

"Right here," Don said, patting his wallet. "Think we'll need it?"

"Who knows, but I don't think we have time for anything else."

As we made our way out, Don asked which vehicle I wanted to take.

"How about mine," I replied. "I have one more trick to show you." As we reached the truck, I reached for a cloth bag that I had hidden under the front seat. In it were a softball-sized red flashing light with a magnetic roof mount base and a cigarette-lighter power adapter.

"Cool," said Don. "Just like on *The Streets of San Francisco*[33]."

"The same. Let's go." With that, we loaded Silver into my truck, positioned the roof light and took off for Cape Breton. As we drove, I explained that my boss was going to try to have Jack meet us along the way. I didn't use the flashing light the whole way, just here and there to keep us moving through traffic congestion and make sure we could make good time on the road. When I did, given that my truck was also a bright red colour, I imagine that people probably took us to be a volunteer fire department responding to a rural call.

We continued to discuss the case as I drove north, and when that dried up Don asked about our police dog training experiences, which naturally led to our work on the Fort McMurray bomb threats the previous year. By the time we crossed the causeway from the mainland onto Cape Breton, I realized that Don had not only done a good job of helping pass the time, but a good job getting me to open up and tell him more about myself. I, on the other hand, had so far learned very little about him. I resolved to change that when I got a chance.

I had thought we might see Jack as we crossed the causeway, as it would be a natural spot from which to watch for us, but there was no sign of him. I tried raising him on the police radio but was only able to contact a confused dispatcher who wondered who I was and what I was doing on a police radio frequency. My explanation that I was an out-of-province officer trying to contact Jack wasn't very convincing, apparently, so I settled for asking them to get Jack to contact me as soon as possible and that in the meantime they could phone my boss in Ottawa for confirmation of my legitimacy.

We'd kept driving through this process, and I eventually learned from the dispatcher that Jack was on another call somewhere. Twenty minutes later this was confirmed by Jack himself, who came on the radio to explain that he'd been on his way to meet me when he'd encountered a serious highway accident and had had to stop to deal with it because there were injured people involved.

Apparently, we'd hit one of those periodic surges in which the quiet tedium of rural policing is interrupted by a rash of events that suddenly have all available officers out on one kind of call or another. In other words, there was no one available to relieve him yet, and he wouldn't be able to leave the scene of the accident for another half hour or so.

I couldn't say too much on the radio - it had only just occurred to me that a radio expert would have no trouble tuning in on our police band if he wanted to. Fortunately, Jack knew what I'd been up to, so I was able to cryptically get across that 'the game is afoot' as Sherlock Holmes used to say, and that my partner and I were heading for the scene of interest. I said that I'd park by the side of the highway and leave my flashing red light on the roof, so he'd be able to find us.

"Seems like we're on our own again," I said to Don as we passed Ingonish Centre. The next village was Ingonish itself.

"What do you want to do?"

"Let's take a quick look at the antique shop and see if anyone is there. If both Marcus and Wilma Light are in town, then I think we should probably just stay well back and observe until we can get reinforcements."

Don agreed and when we entered the village, I stopped well back from the Oceanside Antiques Store. It was early evening now, but there was no light on outside the store, no vehicles parked in front, and it wasn't obvious that any inside lights were on.

We decided that, with a hooded jacket on, Don would be the least identifiable of us, so he pulled on his jacket and strolled up to the store, walked right by it without appearing to even look at it, then crossed the road and came back to the truck.

"That was quick," I commented, "and from my line of sight you didn't even notice the store as you went by."

"I'm going to choose to take that as a compliment," said Don with a grin. "A compliment, because I saw everything there was to see, including..." he rushed on before I could get another word out, "the piece of paper tacked onto the front door."

"Saying they're closed," I guessed.

"Saying they're closed and written in a rather hasty scrawl if I'm any judge," said Don, with satisfaction.

"So, they've been here and left already. I guess we'd better go see if they're at the weather station."

Just to be thorough, we took a slow drive down the back lane behind the antique store, but everything seemed closed-up, unlighted, and quiet there too. There were no vehicles parked in the vicinity, so we continued on through the village and along the north road. When we reached the usual pull-off spot for hiking to Red Head, there was an older model brown car parked by the side of the road. Pulling up behind it, I made a note of the licence plate number before turning off my headlights. Switching off the engine, I left its parking lights on and then turned on the flashing red light on the roof.

"I guess the time for secrecy is over," I commented as we all got out of the truck. "If they give us the slip, I have their licence plate number and I think we have enough to get a search warrant for their place if we need it."

"My guess is that they can't be more than minutes ahead of us now, so I think we're going to find them at the weather station itself," judged Don.

Don, Silver, and I headed into the woods along the path that Sharon and I had followed almost a month earlier. We were pretty quiet as we carefully hiked along, and when I'd judged that we were getting close to the edge of the woods to the cliff at Red Head, I whispered to Don that I thought we should slow down and approach carefully. At the same time, I patted Silver on the shoulder, and he seemed to understand that we were going to take the last 50 yards or so very carefully.

We covered this last stretch uneventfully, but just before we exited the forest Silver suddenly perked up, sniffed the air a bit, then turned to look at me and gave a very low growl. It wasn't an angry or defensive growl, but rather had a tone of warning.

At this Don and I spread out a bit, but otherwise just kept on approaching as cautiously and silently as we could.

When we reached the clearing, and just before the edge of the cliff, I motioned to Don that the weather station was situated to our left. Don immediately moved ahead and to the left, motioning me to fall back a bit. As he did, I signaled Silver to stay close to me, and the two of us followed.

We weren't far from the weather station at this point and I could soon see that someone was crouched down by one of the cannisters, with their back facing us.

Neither Don nor I said anything, but it was inevitable that one of us would eventually be heard.

I was a bit surprised that, showing no shock or surprise, the figure slowly stood up and calmly turned to face us. Then came the second surprise: it was Wilma!

"We had a feeling that you would come," she said.

11 CONFRONTATION

In order to carry out the duties assigned to them constables
are permitted by law to use the minimum amount of force
necessary to cope with a given situation. Still, the discharge
of firearms in the line of duty amounts to such violent force
that they must only be resorted to in the most extreme cases...
A constable may use a weapon in self-defence, if in carrying
out their legal duty, their life is endangered by the unlawful
act of another person and no less violent defence is adequate
or available.

"R.C.M.P. CONSTABLES' MANUAL." OTTAWA

I shot a man once. Shot him twice actually.

*I hadn't wanted to. I'd been trying to talk him down, wanting to give him
every possible chance to surrender, but he'd already taken several shots at me.
When he had shot Silver, I'd fired in return. Recovering, he'd raised his rifle
again and aimed it at Silver. Then his body shifted, and I sensed that he was
going to fire again. Once again, I'd yelled "Don't do it!" but this time I didn't
wait for him to fire first. I fired before he could get off another shot and kill
Silver.*

My shots hit him both times, once in each leg, which is what had finally grounded him and caused him to drop his weapon. The biggest question Assistant Commissioner Macleod had, was why I'd shot this fellow in the legs and hadn't aimed for the heart? Bob, for his part, had marvelled at my shooting accuracy, considering that I'd only been armed with a snub-nose revolver and had been shooting under extreme duress!

Sheepishly, I'd explained the embarrassing truth, which was that I'd actually aimed for his torso. The centre of his torso in fact. I really wasn't trying to kill him, I was trying to stop him. Aiming dead-centre was simply so that I'd have the best odds of actually hitting him at all, which was the way I'd been taught. It was fortunate for me because I really wasn't that good a shot, and it was just a fluke - two flukes, in fact - that I'd ended up shooting him in both legs. My explanation had produced howls of laughter from Bob and the Assistant Commissioner, but they clearly approved, and both hastened to tell me that they were still impressed that I'd been able to stop our suspect before he'd been able to hurt or kill anyone else. Our suspect was convicted on several charges and is serving a life sentence in prison.

The episode left me with distinctly mixed feelings about easy-to-conceal but inaccurate weapons.

***

Now, roughly a year later, here I was in a somewhat similar situation.

"Where's Marcus?"

I said it loudly enough for Wilma to hear, but it was Don that I'd wanted to warn. If Wilma was here, I was suddenly certain that Marcus would not be far away.

Don had heard me, but he was clearly on the same page I was, and he'd immediately drawn a small pistol of some kind that he must previously have had concealed in his clothing somewhere. As he was drawing his gun, he repeated my question. "Where is Marcus, Wilma? He wouldn't have left you to do this by himself!"

"You are quite correct, young man," came a voice from behind me. It was Marcus.

"Everyone should move very slowly as I am feeling a bit nervous right now," continued Marcus, raising an ugly looking Luger and pointing it in Don's and my general direction. I suppose that "ugly looking" is an odd description to apply to a gun, but that's how it seemed to me at the time.

Although Marcus had said he was feeling nervous, his voice was entirely calm and his diction was precise.

"... and where is that rather large dog of yours?" Marcus continued.

"I don't know," I answered truthfully. Silver had quietly faded away into the forest, but I knew that he wouldn't be far away.

"It would be best for both of you if you drop the gun and surrender to us," said Don.

"You would be from some part of the military – am I right?" Don nodded.

"And you are?" Marcus asked, looking at me.

"Police, RCMP," I replied, "Don's right, it would be best for both of you to drop that gun. I honestly don't know whether either of you would even be charged with anything, but you can't point a gun at us, and we can't let you send that message out."

"I am afraid that it is too late for us, my dear. I have been working in the service of the Fatherland since 1942... thirty-five years now, and I'm afraid that I'm too old to change my ways now. Besides, we haven't even lost yet. We can just send our message out and then leave the country as quietly as we entered so many years ago."

"Alex is right, Marcus," said Don, raising both his voice and his pistol and aiming the gun in Marcus' direction. "You need to drop that gun – right now."

BLAM!

Without blinking, Marcus had immediately fired. I startled and simultaneously realized that I hadn't been hit, so I turned to look back at Don, who had dropped his gun and was trying to hold back the blood that was oozing between the fingers he had clasped around his right arm.

I think I sensed Silver's motion, even before I heard the sounds of him running nearby in the forest.

"Stop your dog or I will shoot him too," said Marcus, still very calm and precise.

"Silver!" I exclaimed loudly. Sure enough, he hadn't missed a thing and was in the woods directly in line with Marcus. He'd already started running towards Marcus, probably as soon as he heard the gunshot, and we could all hear the sound of him sliding as he immediately halted his running motion. I told Silver to stay where he was, and thankfully he listened to me.

"I don't know how long I can keep him at bay Marcus, but if you shoot me, he'll tear your arm off, and if you shoot him, I'll throw you over the cliff myself."

"I believe you," said Marcus. "Just stand where you are for now and no one else needs to get hurt." Then, "Wilma! Pick up that little gun of his and throw it over the cliff."

Wilma, who had quietly approached, just nodded, picked up Don's gun, and did as Marcus had instructed.

"Now then, here's what we're all going to do. You two just stand still and you, young lady, keep that dog where he is. Wilma will go back and send our message out. We almost had everything ready when you came along, and it won't take long to send the message out, then – if you cooperate - we can all leave peacefully."

"Why should we believe you?" I asked. "Are you just going to let us go after shooting Don and threatening Silver and I?"

"Now, now," Marcus admonished, "the very fact that you are here means our cover here is compromised. That means our work here is ended. As long as Wilma and I can walk away, we will quietly leave the country and you will never see or hear of us again, and that will be the end of it."

"You sound pretty confident," I commented.

"Of course. As you now know, I have been working in your country for a very long time. It was inevitable that I would be discovered some day, and I have done my best to prepare accordingly. I have several contingency plans for our exit, which I won't disclose to you. I noted that your friend here failed to identify himself, but I judge him to be a soldier ..."

Then, looking directly at Don, "don't bother to deny it, it shows plainly on your face. As a soldier, you will appreciate that when my mission is accomplished it is my duty to return home. In my situation, you would do the same. I have no desire to hurt either of you any further, so if you're prepared to be civilized about all this then we can soon all go on our way, and you will be able to go and tell your superiors that you have eliminated the enemy's transmitting station, but that the clever spies got away. They will be sufficiently pleased, I think."

"You're very clever," I replied. "If we're all going to be so civilized about this, do you mind if I help tend to my friend's bleeding arm? I have a bandage on my leg that will do him more good than it will me right now."

"Go right ahead," said Marcus, expansively. He felt that he was in complete control now, and clearly enjoying it. "Wilma, you go and send our message, while I keep an eye on these three."

Other than reminding Silver to stay put, I didn't waste any time going over to Don and prying his hand away from his arm, so I could have a look at his arm. There was a small, bleeding hole where the bullet had gone in, of course and a larger and ragged exit hole on the other side of his arm. It was the exit hole that was really bleeding badly.

"The bullet's gone right through Don, but we're still going to need to put your arm in a sling." Don had brought his light cotton pullover with him, tied around his waist, and I usually carried a woman's handkerchief in my pocket. Pulling out my handkerchief, I placed it over Don's entrance wound and got him to hold it in place while I pulled off the bandage I'd been wearing on one leg – the one that held my Derringer. Quickly slipping the Derringer into the pocket of my Bermuda Shorts, I used the tape to secure my makeshift bandage on Don's arm, then used his pullover to build a makeshift sling to support his arm. This done I turned to face Marcus and took my Derringer out in the same motion.

"Last warning Marcus – drop the gun!"

He laughed, of course. I knew he would.

So... there we were, and just like in my *déjà vu* moment, I was outgunned. Just like a high-powered rifle had had the advantage over my snub-nose revolver back in Alberta a year earlier, now Max's 9-mm semi-automatic Luger pistol had the advantage over my two-chamber Derringer.

Except that it was worse than that.

It would have been somewhat of a standoff, except that the only advantage I had left was surprise - so I used it. I aimed and pulled the trigger.

There was an audible 'click' sound.

If Marcus laughed politely before, he was even more amused now. "You went to all the trouble to hide and carry that thing all this time and didn't even remember to load it? No wonder there aren't any other women in the RCMP!" he exclaimed.

While Marcus had his little joke and final comments, I'd continued to point the Derringer at him, with what I'd hoped was a suitably rueful, embarrassed expression.

Now, as Marcus tensed to pull the Luger's trigger, I pulled the trigger of my Derringer again and fired. It may have been a tiny little gun, but a .38 Special bullet fired at short range can easily kill.

Marcus dropped like a rock, having immediately dropped his Luger so he could press both hands over his chest on a spot centred on, and to the right of his breastbone.

"Not bad," I thought, clinically, serious but probably not life-threatening.

On the ground, writhing in pain, Marcus had to force his next words out: "What happened?"

"It wasn't that I didn't load the gun," I explained, "but it only had two chambers. I was taught to always leave the chamber with the hammer over it empty, to make sure that the gun doesn't go off accidentally if it's ever dropped. In this case, that made a two-shot Derringer into a one-shot Derringer."

As I said this I'd run over to Marcus, not to help with his wound — not yet anyway — but to recover his Luger, which I immediately tossed to Don. Silver had immediately come to my side to make sure I was OK, and I gave him a reassuring pat on the shoulder.

"Can you shoot with your left hand?" I asked Don.

"Well enough," he replied, grimly, and turned to go pull Wilma away from the transmitting station.

"The message hadn't been sent yet," he called back over his shoulder. "She'd just lined up the perforated tape though, so it was a close call."

While Don kept an eye on Wilma, I helped with first aid for Marcus. As I was working on stopping the bleeding from his chest, I heard a dull sound in the distance that eventually resolved itself into the '*thump, thump, thump*' sounds of a large helicopter approaching.

Before long, what started out as a barely discernable thumping had developed into a blasting roar as a Sea King[34] helicopter suddenly popped-up into sight over the edge of the cliff. It had clearly come along the coast, low and out of our sight and mostly out of hearing as it approached. As the helicopter rose up above cliff level, its crew switched on a powerful searchlight. It had been getting quite dark before this, but now we were all bathed in an intense, broad beam of light. Without bothering to land, the helicopter pilot simply hovered a foot from the ground and several MPs in combat fatigues hopped out, with their sidearms drawn.

The MPs naturally went to Don first, and after a few words the senior among them, a Sergeant, came over to me and told me that they were there to provide any assistance I might need. Thanking him, I asked for whatever first aid supplies they might have so we could get Don and Marcus properly bandaged.

By the time that was taken care of, Jack appeared from the forest path, also with his gun drawn. He had seen my truck parked with its red light flashing and had just pulled-up behind it when he heard the first gunshot. Hearing that, he'd first called for backup, and then come running.

We found out later that the timing of the helicopter's arrival had been a bit of a fluke. Don's call to his boss before we'd left Halifax had set in motion a chain of events that led to a helicopter being detached from a navy frigate. It had picked up the MPs and headed directly for our area. They were originally going to land on one of the nearby beaches, but Jack's call for backup had also been relayed to the military, who had alerted the helicopter crew.

With the hammering sound of the nearby helicopter, we couldn't really talk much – it was more like terse yelling at each other, but I was able to satisfy myself that Don was going to be OK.

"The bullet wound is nothing," Don had yelled. "I just about had heart failure when I heard the hammer go 'click' on the empty chamber in your Derringer. I thought it was a misfire, and we were all going to either be shot or pushed over the cliff!"

Telling him that I'd come and see him in Halifax as soon as I could, I stepped back so the MPs could take Don and Marcus by helicopter to one of the hospitals in Halifax. Meanwhile, Jack and Silver and I took charge of Wilma and headed back through the forest to our vehicles.

Before we left Red Head, however, I went back to the old weather station. I wanted to disable it without destroying anything, so in the end, I simply used my UDT knife to cut the cables running to and from the cannister that contained the tape-reading machine and carried Marcus and Wilma's tape and the entire cannister out with me.

When we reached our vehicles where they'd been parked alongside the highway, Jack radioed in and learned that instructions had come from Ottawa to arrest and hold both Marcus and Wilma on charges under the Official Secrets Act. Jack took care of that part, leaving Silver and I free for the moment.

I'd wanted to head back to Halifax to see Don, but recognizing the early signs of exhaustion in me, and knowing that after all the excitement there would be a low following the adrenalin surge I'd been operating on, Jack wisely talked me into coming back to the detachment with him to get some food and sleep first.

I thought it was ironic that while our efforts had led to the capture and arrest of Marcus and Wilma, Silver and I had spent the night sleeping in a cell at the Baddeck RCMP detachment.

At least the door to our cell wasn't locked.

12 AFTERMATH

By the time Silver and I got back to Halifax the next day, Don had been treated and released from the hospital with orders to stay home and rest for the day. We visited him at his apartment, and it was a relief to learn that the bullet had only grazed the bone before it had gone the rest of the way through his arm. Whereas I had expected to see his arm in a cast and supported by a sling, he was simply bandaged and still taking pain killers. Not bad, considering what might have happened.

I'd been wondering what I'd do for however long it took the military cryptology people to decode the intercepted messages, but I needn't have worried. While we were discussing the previous day's adventure – our second life-or-death adventure already, Don received a phone call from one of his colleagues in military intelligence. Once he found out what it was about he put it on his speakerphone, so we could both listen. Don's cryptology colleagues had finally broken Marcus' code!

Since Don still had trouble writing, due to his injury, I reached for a pen and paper and took notes. The intercepted messages were short and simple, containing only the dates, times, and places for meetings. The implication was that there was a foreign agent, or agents, in place in the region, and/or coming and going through Halifax. The current working assumption was that Marcus was not actively involved in such meetings, but simply a messaging relay. That should mean that the meeting referred in to the latest message should still go ahead.

The next news was about the latest message, the one that Don had intercepted while we were on the boat together. It specified that the meeting would be "15:00, 06.07.1977, by the anchor, Point Pleasant Park." In other words, at 3 pm July 6th in Point Pleasant Park.

"'By the anchor' can only mean somewhere close to that huge anchor monument from the aircraft carrier[35]," I concluded.

"That's what we think too," confirmed Don's colleague on the phone.

"But July 6th is tomorrow!" Don exclaimed. "That's not much time to prepare anything."

"Right, I'm supposed to tell both of you to call your bosses ASAP for instructions," concluded Don's colleague.

Thanking him, I hung up the phone and stared at Don for a few moments.

"What would you do if you were in our bosses' shoes?" I asked Don.

"Depends on whether they want to arrest these people or just follow them, I guess. Sometimes the game is to learn who the agents are and then just keep an eye on them, sometimes it's to grab them and try to turn them in to double agents, and other times it's just to arrest them before they flee and try to get them convicted and put away."

There was little point in speculating any further, so we decided I should call Bob first. I reached Bob right away and let him know that we were on speakerphone and that Don was with me.

"Excellent," said Bob. "Hi, Don."

"Hello, Sir."

"I'm glad you're both together because I just got off the phone with Don's boss and we have come up with a plan. Congratulations on foiling Marcus' attempt to send a new message. We're going to work on the assumption that the previous message is still valid, and that Marcus wasn't going to be part of the meeting itself. Unfortunately, that doesn't give us much time to organize a reception committee!"

"We were thinking the same thing here."

"OK then, here's the thing: under other circumstances, we might just put a surveillance team on each of the people that meet. It will likely be just two people. In this case, however, we want to know what they're exchanging at these meetings. What we want to do is have a surveillance team ready to follow the sender, wherever they go. For that person we have time on our side, so we'll use a plainclothes team and have them just follow and report. The recipient we want to be arrested so we can find out who they are, where they came from, and what they're receiving. For that person, we need an arrest team."

"Can we help?" Don and I both asked at the same time.

"That's the spirit!" said Bob, approvingly. "Yes, you can. We don't have time to organize a big team, and we have to send in the smallest team we can anyway to minimize the risk that our two suspects spot something unusual, get spooked, and abort the meeting. We have three Security Service people attached to H Division[36], and we'll have them be the surveillance team for the sender. You two can go meet them at H Division headquarters tomorrow morning."

"That's it?" I asked.

"Oh no," replied Bob. "I'm detaching Jack from the pretense of his temporary assignment at the Baddeck Detachment and sending him down to act as a liaison between you two and the Halifax Regional Police. He'll be driving down tomorrow morning and you'll be able to meet him in the afternoon sometime. He'll have his highway patrol car, so you can contact him by radio. Now, Don doesn't have the authority to make a civilian arrest, but I've formally requested his assistance from the Canadian Forces which gives him fairly wide latitude in how he assists you and Jack. What I want you, Alex, or Jack to do is arrest the recipient and seize whatever it is that the sender passes to him, OK?"

"OK," echoed Don and I together.

"All right then, one more thing. I want you to go in uniform. The surveillance team will go in plain clothes, and their job is to watch, not to interfere with anything. If we're lucky, our two suspects will meet, exchange something, then separate. When they're out of sight of each other the surveillance team can shadow, and the arrest team can move in. The arrest team will be Jack and a couple of people from H Division. I want you two there as a backup for the arrest team. If things go wrong and there's a chase, I want you to be instantly recognizable to police and civilians alike, OK?"

"OK," we repeated.

"Right then, when you meet up with Jack he can introduce you to the H Division people. Good luck!"

After hanging-up Don and I looked at each other for a moment.

"Wow, this could get dangerous again Alex," said Don.

"Well, so far in my career I've been sexually harassed, trapped in a mine shaft, shot at, and shipwrecked. Silver here has been marooned, left to die, shot, and dumped into the ocean – which he hates with a passion. We've survived a lot together. Maybe we'll survive this too. Besides, what else could possibly go wrong?"

"Bite your tongue!" responded Don. The words and his tone sounded so much like me that we both had a good laugh. With nothing else to do but wait for the moment, we decided to go out for dinner and then to meet the next day for lunch.

***

The next day was the day of the 'big spy meeting,' as Don and I thought of it. Our lunch *rendezvous* meeting was at the same Harvey's Restaurant in Dartmouth at which we'd originally met. This time I was in uniform, wearing my black tactical uniform – which I favoured for working in the field with Silver – and my service revolver, which made a change from the little Derringer I'd been carrying around all summer.

"Now you look like a police officer – and serious business too!" Don quipped half-admiringly and half-teasingly.

"You don't look like anyone to trifle with yourself," I observed, noting that Don was in uniform again, but this time, instead of a Naval Lieutenant's dress uniform he had on camouflage fatigues with Captain's bars, an MP armband, and a sidearm. "I see that you're a Captain again today… who are you really?"

Don sighed and thought for a moment. "I have a strange job and sometimes I get confused myself. I started out as a CELE officer like I told you, but it was originally in the Air Force, not the Navy. I really am a Captain, but other than that I'm often whatever I need to be depending on what mission I've been assigned. I lose track of who I really am sometimes, but when we were on the island trying to survive together, that was the real me. It was scary, but I felt grounded, if you know what I mean, for the first time in a long time. Seems strange to say it out loud, but I'm glad we went through that together."

"I am too, but let's not do it again for a while, OK?"

"OK by me," Don agreed – "let's eat."

By unspoken agreement, we avoided talking about work for a while and just enjoyed munching on our burgers together. It struck me, while we were eating how comfortable I had become with Don. I'd been on dates before and had a boyfriend for several years in high school, but this was different. We'd evolved from being colleagues to partners, to friends and it occurred to me that Don was rapidly becoming best-friend material. This was a new experience for me and I wondered where it might lead.

***

After lunch, I was able to raise Jack on the police radio and we arranged to meet him and the other Security Service people at H Division headquarters. I found them pretty reserved, almost secretive, and quite aloof, but I didn't have to like them I just had to be able to work with them. I did, however, take the precaution of introducing them to Silver so he could register their scent and know that they were on our side. The briefing was fairly straightforward, since the plan was for Don, Jack, Silver, and I to stay in the background but be available to help catch our 'recipient suspect' if necessary, while the others covertly tailed the 'sender suspect.'

After the briefing, there wasn't a lot of time for waiting as we had to be in position long before the specified meeting time of 3 pm.

We'd been issued hand-held VHF radios, and Don, Jack, Silver and I took position hiding out in my big red truck in a back corner of one of the upper-level parking lots. There were closer places to park down by the harbor-front, but we didn't want to be spotted by either of our suspects.

When 3 pm arrived, it wasn't long before we heard "someone's approaching the bench" over the radio, presumably referring to one of the park benches that was near the anchor memorial. It seemed like an eternity but was probably only a couple of minutes before this was followed by "here comes number two."

After that, the pace of events picked-up considerably.

"Shit!" we heard someone say. "Did someone break cover?" then "Damn."

"Jack are you there?"

"Right here," Jack confirmed.

"Our two suspects met all right, but only briefly. Something spooked them, and they've bolted. They did exchange something, and most of our team is going to follow the sender. The other guy left a sweater behind, so we'll leave someone here to show you in case your dog can get the scent and track him."

"OK," Jack replied, "we're coming now."

With the need for secrecy gone, I threw my red flashing light up on the roof of my truck, hit the gas, and simply drove down the walking path towards the monument. You weren't supposed to drive on the walking path, of course, but it was wide enough for the park maintenance vehicles, so it was wide enough for me. There weren't many people on the path, so I made good time getting down to the monument and we quickly spotted one of my Security Service colleagues standing by a nearby park bench.

Sure enough, in his rush to get away, our recipient had conveniently left a grey sweater behind. I let Silver register a good series of sniffs while Don and Jack wrote down the suspect's description. It sounded like it was a middle-aged male wearing everyday clothes - browns and beiges in colour - that could just as easily denote a tourist or Halifax resident. The key news for us was that he was carrying a significantly heavy gym bag – so that, at least, would stand out.

It was Silver's turn now, and he led us along the beaches, across the waterfront parking lot, and past the container ship terminal, heading in the direction of downtown. As we followed, Jack radioed in the recent events and asked to have the Halifax police keep an eye out for anyone in the harbor-front area matching our suspect's description.

Silver did his usual tracking routine, sweeping left and right, frequently stopping to sniff around. He didn't seem to have much trouble following the scent through, as he only occasionally lost the track and had to sweep more broadly before finding it again. As he continued to lead us towards the downtown area, we passed the big grain elevators, the historic Pier 21 Immigration Dock, and then a small marina and the docks for tug boats and the Harbor Pilot boats. Now we were in the most popular walking area for tourists and locals alike, and it became much harder for Silver to keep track of the scent while navigating around all the people that were out for a stroll and the inevitable children and other dogs that wanted to approach and say "hi" to him. We all persevered as best we could, however, and something like forty minutes into our tracking, Jack suddenly exclaimed "Look there," and pointed straight ahead.

Sure enough, we could just make out the back of someone matching our suspect's description and carrying a bag of some kind. Jack volunteered to break off to our left and try to run up ahead along Lower Water Street, in parallel with our suspect's current heading. Jack was the runner among us, so it made sense for him to break away while Don stayed with Silver and I in direct pursuit.

Our suspect hadn't noticed us yet and apparently knew better than to frequently turn and look back over his shoulder. Jack would need some time to sweep up along the parallel street, so we let Silver continue with his tracking. Since our suspect was trying to blend in with the crowd he was walking at the rate of a leisurely stroll, so we were able to narrow the gap between us.

If it was indeed our recipient, then it was inevitable that he would eventually look behind him. Sure enough, he soon stopped to look at a local vendor's display and gave a very casual glance back the way he had come. His body language immediately changed, showing that he'd spotted us and correctly interpreted our presence. He was good though. Without otherwise seeming to show any alarm, he simply resumed his former route, but he increased his pace. Silver was ready to race on ahead, but I told him to stay and keep pace with Don and me.

"Where will he go?" I asked Don. "He could try for the ferry, but we'd just get on it too."

"Watch for a tour boat or a sailboat that's about to leave the dock," Don suggested. "He might try jumping on one that's just leaving!"

Don and I increased our pace now, to make sure that we could keep our suspect in sight, and Don radioed a warning to Jack, telling him that our suspect was nearing the Queen's Landing Market and might get lost in the crowd. Jack said "OK," and that he'd approach the market from the north side, while we approached from the south side. With the harbor to our right, that would still leave the west side unguarded, however.

We'd no sooner agreed to this than our suspect reached the market and melted into the crowd. At this Don and I broke into an all-out run and, as we hadn't been far away, reached the market only about thirty seconds behind our suspect. Forced to slow down by the crowd, I was able to catch my breath and suggest that Don stay with me and let Silver find him.

Silver, for his part, knew exactly what we were doing and led us on a zig-zag route through the crowd. He couldn't have had much scent to go on, but he seemed always to find a rough trail to follow, led us to the east side of the market square, and then came to a halt looking directly ahead to a market stall that was selling brightly coloured scarves. At first, I didn't see why he had stopped, but on second glance there was our suspect holding a woman in front of him. He had one arm around her, with the gym bag still clutched in his hand. His other hand held a gun, and the gun was aimed at us.

"That's close enough," the man said.

Silver and I had already stopped. I wondered at first why Don had stepped behind me, but I was answered by the sound of him quietly relaying information to Jack on his radio.

Our suspect guessed at the truth as well, saying "Tell your colleague to come out where I can see him and to drop the radio." Don came and stood beside me and placed his radio on the ground.

"Good. Now, here's what we're going to do. This lady and I are going to find a boat to take us out in the harbor. If you stay out of our way, I'll release her further along the harbor and no one needs to get hurt. OK?"

"You'll never get away with this." As I said this I realized that the words could have come out of a Hollywood movie, but they needed to be said.

"I'll take my chances, thank you," replied our suspect, and nudged into motion the woman he'd grabbed.

As the two of them moved back towards the docks, Jack arrived at the edge of the crowd to our suspect's left. Telling him to stop, our suspect repeated the instructions he'd just given us. Seeing that he was momentarily distracted, I made a sweeping motion with my arm and Silver melted into the crowd to our right.

Keeping a grip on the gym bag and the woman from the market, our suspect backed the two of them slowly but surely towards the docks while trying to keep an eye on Jack, Don, and I. He seemed to have forgotten about Silver, or maybe he hadn't realized that Silver was with us. A hush had fallen over the other shoppers, who seemed to have melted away with the sudden appearance of a man brandishing a gun. That was just as well, as it cleared the field for us.

To the onlookers, it must have seemed like a movie set, but Jack, Don, and I were all too aware of the potential for people to get hurt or killed if someone made a wrong move.

As luck would have it, no sooner had our suspect and his hostage reached the docks again than an empty tour boat swung alongside, probably in preparation for another load of sight-seers. As a deck-hand hopped onto the pier to tie up the boat, our suspect yelled to him to stay where he was. Our suspect was close enough that by the time the deck-hand had completed a double-take, there was a gun waving in his face, causing him to hesitate even further.

The deck-hand's confusion worked to our advantage, as our suspect now had to slow down and explain what he wanted to be done.

This was our chance!

I yelled "Run to the Mountie!" to the woman, pointing to Jack who was off to one side.

Fortunately, she had the courage and presence of mind to pull away and run for Jack, causing a moment of confusion for our suspect. We would have only another second before he decided that the deck-hand could just as well be his new hostage, and I used that second to yell, "Silver, get the gun!"

Silver heard the urgency in my voice and, almost instantaneously, there was a greyish-white blur and a yell of pain from our suspect. In the blink of an eye, Silver had his jaws clamped on our suspect's arm, between the forearm and wrist. Our suspect was still gamely holding onto the gun, but with Silver's jaws fully engaged on his arm and all of Silver's considerable weight dragging it down, he wasn't likely to be able to shoot at anything vulnerable. Only a few seconds behind Silver, Don and I grabbed our suspect as well, just as he was trying to use his other arm to toss the gym bag out into the harbour.

It didn't take long for us to disarm and arrest him. Jack had called for reinforcements, who took him into custody for us. Jack also took down the names and addresses of the woman from the market and the man from the tour boat, and he made sure that they were both OK.

When we opened the gym bag, we found several reels of black and white 35-mm film and a bunch of pieces of metal in varying sizes and shapes.

"Any idea what these are?" I asked Don.

"No, but if I had to guess, I'd say that they are samples of metal alloys from one of the Cape Breton heavy water plants. There really isn't anything else in this region that would interest a foreign country in our metallurgy – but nuclear secrets are always a hot commodity. The DREA[37] folks will be able to tell us for sure."

So, that was it. It was a bit of an anticlimax after Don's and Silver's and my adventure on the cliff at Red Head, but still quite exciting. We had accomplished at least part of our objective by capturing one of the suspects and his stuff and, of course, we had uncovered Marcus' and Wilma's operation as well.

Later that day we learned that the 'sending suspect' had raced deep into the park and managed to elude the officers that were chasing him. The Security Service would continue working to figure out who he was and probably start watching him for a while to get a better sense of the extent of his activities.

13 LOOSE ENDS

The receiving suspect that Don, Jack, Silver, and I had caught was debriefed by a combined team from Military Intelligence and the RCMP Security Service. He admitted to being an East German agent and provided more insight into how their message transfers worked. When one of their locally-based sources was ready with new industrial materials to sell, they would get a message to Marcus, who would, in turn, send out meeting dates from his hidden, low-power transmitter. The messages could be received on any shortwave radio receiver that was in the general area of the Atlantic Provinces or U.S. New England States, as long as the receiving person had a means of decoding, or at least recording, the message burst. Such receivers were sometimes on military vessels, like submarines, but were more often on innocuous vessels like commercial freighters.

In the case of our receiving suspect, he had come to Canada only the day before our meeting, on a container ship, and had received the message with the meeting particulars while still at sea. The container ships generally only docked for a day – just long enough to unload/load their cargo – then left port the next day. This is why careful coordination of the meetings was needed. They also had to be flexible, because the container ships don't follow a rigid schedule – sometimes they arrived every week, but sometimes only every other week. If we hadn't intercepted him, he would have boarded the same container ship the night of the hand-off and the ship would have been gone the following morning.

I hadn't realized that container ships carried passengers but, apparently, they do – usually up to ten passengers at a time – in nice, but not luxurious accommodations. After leaving Halifax, a typical itinerary would have the ship go, in succession, to New York, Norfolk, Savannah, Charleston, and through the Suez Canal to various ports in Asia. Our suspect could disembark in any of those cities. If in a hurry it would be New York, but to avoid having a regular pattern it would often be one of the other U.S. ports, after which he'd simply board a regular passenger liner for the transatlantic crossing home. The reason for choosing ships was simple: no metal detectors or X-raying of passenger baggage, and generally lax customs and immigration checks compared with other means of crossing in and out of Canada.

He admitted that the Soviet Bloc nations were keenly interested in Canada's CANDU[38] nuclear reactor and heavy water production technologies and had been acquiring pieces of the technology for several years. They already had the necessary scientific knowledge of course. What they wanted was the practical know-how, hence their interest in operating plant specifications and procedures, specific equipment, and specific material requirements such as specialized metal alloys – thus the metal samples he had been trying to smuggle out.

In the end, he was threatened but not charged with any crimes. Bob and his counterpart talked him into becoming a double-agent for them. After making a copy of the spools of film and photographing the pieces of metal alloy, they let him take them home with him. I didn't ever hear how it all turned out in the end. That is, whether our suspect continued to work as a double-agent, was eventually turned into a triple-agent by the other side, or whether something worse happened to him.

I did ask Bob why they bothered with such elaborate measures when they could just send films and samples out in diplomatic bags from their embassy in Ottawa (even though this kind of use of diplomatic bags was forbidden). Bob explained that many of the foreign embassies in Ottawa have intelligence agents, who could be anyone from a military attaché to the Ambassador, but it was complicated.

"We generally know who the intelligence agents are, and we watch them carefully," Bob explained. "By the same token, they know that we know who they are, and we know that they know.

So, they have to be very careful about the risks that they take, and sometimes we intercept their diplomatic bags and search them, even though that too is forbidden by diplomatic convention."

This conversation with Bob did not inspire me to get further involved in foreign intelligence work!

***

The story of our sending suspect was later resolved by the Security Service. The plain-clothes officers had never found him in Point Pleasant Park, but the spools of the film contained images of plans and specifications for parts of our heavy water plants. As secret-classified documents, they were individually numbered, so it didn't take long to figure out who had access to them, and of those people who made periodic trips to Halifax – including the date of the most recent meeting, which we had interrupted.

Bob and his Military Intelligence had some fun with this suspect, who they also convinced to work for them, and through whom they sent years-worth of slightly altered plans, specifications, and operating instructions. I don't know if it's true or not, but I was told by a colleague that if another country followed all those altered plans and instructions, that critical parts of the processing plant would spin out of balance until they self-destructed.

***

Marcus and Wilma seemed almost relieved to be done with their espionage activities and told us a fascinating story. Marcus Light's real name had been Max Lichte, and on October 25, 1942, he had been put ashore by German Navy U-boat – number U-687. Along with the crew, he had helped carry the components for *Wetter-Funkgerät Land (Weather Radio for Land) number one, or WFL-1,* the automated weather station, up to the top of the cliff at Red Head, where he assembled it and got everything working. After that was done, the U-boat moved south along the coast, and one of the submarine's dinghies put Marcus and his suitcases ashore on Ingonish Beach at 3 am. After waiting by the side of the road until dawn, he had been able to hitch a ride with local fisherman, claiming to be a travelling salesman. He briefly established himself at Keltic Lodge and later moved to Ingonish. During the war, his mission was simply to remain under cover and maintain the weather station – nothing more.

After the end of the Second World War, however, the East German government had asked Marcus to stay in place, convert the weather station to a message sending station, and be available to transmit encrypted messages for them from time to time. Feeling that such was his duty, he had agreed and later sent for his girlfriend Willie (Wilhelmina). Willie had agreed, and the East German government had arranged for her to be smuggled into the country. They were provided with forged documents showing their names to be Marcus and Wilma Light and had set-up a home, and base of operations, in their antique store in Ingonish. Meanwhile, the official records back in Germany were altered to show that Max and Wilhelmina had gone missing during the war and were presumed dead.

Marcus had certainly been successful in that his careful sending of short-burst, low-power messages from the former automatic weather station had worked well and without detection for nearly 35 years! I learned that Military Intelligence had previously tracked foreign agents to Halifax but then their trails had always run cold. They had suspected that someone must have been radioing signals to ships approaching the harbour. They had assumed the source would be in Halifax but had never intercepted any such signals, leaving them mystified. No one had considered that the transmitter might be as far away as Cape Breton, much less a hold-over from the Second World War.

I had mixed feelings about Marcus and Wilma. When I first knew them, they seemed to be genuinely nice people. Wilma, in particular, reminded me of one of my favourite Aunts: always cheerful, friendly, and welcoming. I had experienced another side of their characters on the cliff at Red Head, where they had shot Don, threatened to shoot Silver and I, and I really don't think either one of them would have hesitated to throw us all over the cliff. Even during the debriefing with our Security Service and Military Intelligence colleagues, Marcus failed to show any remorse whatsoever, and Wilma's only regret was that the two of them had never really gotten married so many years before.

They were charged with attempted murder and a few other things, but in the end, our government simply deported them to Germany with the suggestion that they focus on retirement in the 'old country' and a stern warning to count themselves lucky. As far as I know, that's exactly what they did.

I still have the brass model diver's helmet that I had bought from them.

***

Before leaving Halifax, I visited Sharon and her boss to thank them for their help and support – especially Sharon, who had become a friend. Her boss was gracious and fascinated rather than irritated by my deception, and I told him as much of the truth as I could about my adventure – which wasn't much, really, but seemed to satisfy him.

Just before Jack left to return to his main posting in Alberta, I had Sharon over for dinner one day, so she could visit with all of us: Jack, Don, and of course Silver and I. It was brief but very nice. A lot, in fact, like a family reunion and it gave me another of my *déjà vu* remembrances, recalling to my mind how hard it had been to leave the new friends I had made on my previous three assignments – the most recent ones in Fort McMurray and Innisfail, Alberta, and the one before that in Radium City, Saskatchewan. I resolved to stay in touch with all these new friends as best I could.

I knew that I didn't have to thank Jack for his help, but I did anyway. He said that he'd enjoyed his time as a 'spook' in Atlantic Canada but that he was looking forward to getting back to regular policing back in Alberta. We were both sure that our paths would cross again, so we only had to say: "Good-bye for now."

And Don?

I had to clean everything out of the lab I'd been using at Dalhousie, and after all our adventures there was a bunch of paperwork to do of course, so Silver and I had to stay on in Halifax for several more days. On the first of these, after our capture of the recipient suspect, Don had come over to my place for a visit and supper, which had become a familiar pattern with us, but this time he seemed unaccountably nervous.

"What's eating you, anyway?" I eventually asked.

"Well, I want to ask you something, but I'm feeling a bit embarrassed," he replied, rather sheepishly, which wasn't like Don at all.

"Embarrassed? Don, we've faced death together and seen each other naked, what could possibly be embarrassing?"

"Well… I was wondering if you would like to go out for dinner with me tomorrow night … but not as colleagues, … on a date?"

"A date?"

I pretended to think it over – girls can be cruel sometimes. "Can Silver come along?" Girls can be teases, too.

"Of course!" he replied.

"Then the answer is yes, silly," I replied. That's about when the kissing started.

We went out on dates every night for the rest of the week that I was in Halifax.

***

When Silver and I got back to Ottawa I fulfilled my promise to Scotty and told him what my mission had really been all about, and how his weapons had saved my life – probably twice. He didn't say too much, but I could tell he was pleased.

I also paid a visit to Dr. Alan Grey, my former professor at Carleton University, to thank him for his role in my cover story. When I did, I was surprised and pleased to learn that all my Nova Scotia diving with Sharon had served a greater purpose than just my cover story.

Dr. Grey had had one of his students do the analytical work on my samples and then did all the data analysis himself. It was already known that bivalve molluscs, like mussels and clams, accumulate heavy metals in their soft body tissues. What our measurements showed, was evidence for an inverse correlation between the incidence of heavy metals, particularly cadmium and copper, and the levels of Red Tide toxins in the shellfish tissues. We speculated that the heavy metals were toxic to the algae. Of course, high concentrations of heavy metals in the shellfish tissues would be toxic to humans all by themselves, but our work showed that small heavy metal concentrations could be beneficial, by killing the dangerous algae.

Not only that, but based on all this work, Dr. Grey wrote a scientific paper titled "*The Influence of Red Tide Algae on Heavy Metal Concentrations in Edible Bivalves Found in Coastal Atlantic Canada.*" In the paper, he described our work and its results, proposed a set of mechanisms, recommended further research, and got it all past the journal's referees and editor. That was one pleasant surprise. The second was that he included me as a co-author on the paper! So, I got my first (and probably only) scientific paper publication out of the experience.

Pretty cool!

Reprinted from:

Canadian Journal of Chemistry

The Influence of Red Tide Algae on Heavy Metal Concentrations in Edible Bivalves Found in Coastal Atlantic Canada

ALAN GREY AND ALEXANDRA HOUSTON

Volume 56 ● Number 4 ● 1978
Pages 567-575

National Research
Council Canada

***

While back in Ottawa, I had a few debriefings and conversations with my boss, Bob, and others, which kind of closed the book on my Nova Scotia adventure. At one of the last ones, we were joined by Assistant Commissioner MacLeod, the person that had lured me into the RCMP in the first place. It never ceased to amaze me how the Assistant Commissioner would pop-up, seemingly out of nowhere, just before and just after one of these special projects that I was given. He even hinted that he had another "special assignment" in mind for me but wouldn't disclose it yet.

"You have some annual leave[39] due, so go take a break and we'll talk when you get back to Ottawa," he'd said. "Where do you think you'll go?"

"I'm a bit tempted to just stay here, relax, and enjoy the National Capitol Region a bit, but I've also been thinking about driving to Alaska. It's supposed to be beautiful, and I think that I might try to see if I can discover where Silver was born."

"Well, whatever you decide, give yourself a break from your adventures and decompress a bit," said Bob. "You need to look after yourself, especially since you keep getting into gun battles. If you don't have your wits about you, I'm afraid that one of these times you're going to get hurt!

"I'm not too worried about her," said A/Commr. Macleod. "She's indestructible."

"Hmmm," said Bob, "An Indestructible Mountie."

... Alex and Silver will return,
in *An International Mountie.*

Laurie Schramm

SUMMARY

It is 1977, and a spring hiker on Canada's Cape Breton Island has discovered a strange-looking installation hidden in the forest, on an oceanside cliff. Word of her discovery makes its circuitous way to military intelligence and the RCMP Security Service, where it sets off alarm bells, and Constable Alex Houston and her dog Silver are sent in. They are a unique team since few people know that Alex is the first woman Mountie and Silver, an Alaskan Malamute, looks nothing like a police dog. As they investigate, a technological curiosity from the Second World War turns out to be the centrepiece of something very current, and sinister. As Alex and Silver investigate, this time they will need to be... indestructible.

149

Laurie Schramm

ABOUT THE AUTHOR

Laurie Schramm comes from an RCMP family, grew up while living in the RCMP Barracks (Depot Division) in Regina, Saskatchewan, and spent several summers working as a civilian for the RCMP while in high school and university. Early personal influences included not only the real-life RCMP culture but also Hollywood's versions via such classics as *Rose Marie,* and *Susannah of the Mounties.* Many of the events described in this novel are based on the author's real life, although not necessarily within an RCMP context.

For more information, see Laurier L. Schramm on **Linked** in and:

www.laurieschramm.ca

ENDNOTES

1. In fact, official records still list U-687 as never having been deployed.
2. In exterior dimensions, the submarine was approximately 67 metres in length by just over 6 metres in width.
3. North Atlantic Treaty Organization. A defense alliance of the U.S., Canada, and a number of other countries, formed in 1949.
4. Cathode-ray tube. Very similar in appearance to black and white television screens of the time, except that the displayed images were green on black.
5. The CF Argus was capable of long-range patrols of just over 26 hours when fully armed and loaded.
6. Sound System Underwater Surveillance (SOSUS) was a secret chain of U.S. underwater listening devices placed at strategic locations on the ocean floor. The data was transmitted to shore stations, including one in Nova Scotia.
7. Defence Research Establishment Atlantic (DREA), part of the Canadian Forces' Research and Development Branch, which was reorganized into Defence Research and Development Canada (DRDC) in 2000.
8. "Good Old Raisins and Peanuts," a traditional backpacker's snack, which in Sharon's case was supplemented with candy-covered chocolates.
9. Dalhousie University.
10. A slang term for a licensed amateur radio operator. The term

'ham' seems to have originally been coined by analogy with ham versus professional actors.

11. See *An Inconvenient Mountie* (ISBN: 978-1-9994940-0-1).

12. At this point in time, it was still part of the RCMP. Years later, in 1984, the Security Service was spun-out to create the present-day Canadian Security Intelligence Service (C.S.I.S.).

13. An actual Second-World-War era German *Wetter-Funkgerät Land* automatic weather station, denoted as WFL- 26, was discovered on the Labrador coast in 1977. It is on display in the Canadian War Museum.

14. Heavy water meaning water composed of deuterium and oxygen atoms rather than hydrogen and oxygen atoms.

15. Such weapons were originally called "muff pistols", because their small size enabled them to be carried in a woman's muff.

16. Underwater Demolition Team.

17. Being first occupied in 1915, it was actually 62 years old in 1977.

18. From the French comic series *Astérix le Gaulois*, by R. Goscinny and A. Uderzo.

19. Pyrex™ was a Corning Inc. brand of clear, low-thermal-expansion borosilicate glass that was very popular for laboratory use because it could be heated, cooled, and even handled quite vigorously, without breaking.

20. Buoyancy compensator, or BC, was the prevailing terminology in the 1970s. Eventually, the terms buoyancy compensator device, or BCD, became more common.

21. For SCUBA divers, 'bottom time' is the elapsed time from starting the descent, to the moment of starting the final ascent back to the surface. This does not include the time for the ascent itself, nor decompression stops along the way, if any.

22. See *An Inconspicuous Mountie* (ISBN: 978-1-9994940-2-5).

23. The Cape Islander is Atlantic Canada's signature fishing boat, with its distinctively high, sweeping bow, and a low, flat stern. They are known for their ability to handle rough, rolling seas.

24. Anyone that wasn't born and raised in the Maritimes is considered to be "from away," no matter how long they might stay or live in the Maritimes.

25. Communications and Electronics Engineering.

26. "Bar Clam" is the local name for the Atlantic Surf Clam, *Spisula solidissima*.
27. A large body of mixed fresh and salt water that lies roughly in the centre of Cape Breton Island.
28. Citizens' Band radio. This was officially called the General Radio Service (GRS), but due to the impact of American pop culture of the 1970s, almost everyone referred to CB radios.
29. The same kind of radio scanner that Lenny had used three months earlier on the Canadian Forces CP-107 Argus.
30. It was Friday, July 1, 1977.
31. German U-boats attacked four freighters near Bell Island, Newfoundland. The *SS Saganaga* and *SS Lord Strathcona* were sunk by U-513 on September 5, 1942, and the *SS Rosecastle* and PLM 27 were sunk by U-518 on November 2 of the same year.
32. On November 9, 1942, a German spy was dropped off near New Carlisle, Quebec, by submarine U-518. He was almost immediately caught. His suitcase, which housed a complete radio transmitter, is on display in the RCMP Museum in Regina.
33. A popular police-drama TV series that had just finished its final season.
34. Sikorsky CH-124 Sea Kings are twin-engine, anti-submarine warfare helicopters that were used by Canadian Forces for over 50 years, and which were usually housed on and deployed from destroyers and frigates of the Royal Canadian Navy. Sea Kings were a familiar sight to people in Canada's Atlantic provinces in those days, partly because they frequently assisted with maritime search and rescue operations.
35. The anchor is from *HMCS Bonaventure*.
36. The RCMP Division responsible for federal and provincial policing in Nova Scotia.
37. Defence Research Establishment Atlantic (DREA).
38. CANDU (CANada Deuterium Uranium) is a Canadian pressurized heavy water reactor design used to generate electric power. The word deuterium refers to the deuterium oxide (heavy water) that is used to moderate the nuclear fission reaction, and the word uranium refers to the uranium that is used as the fuel.
39. Vacation.

Laurie Schramm

ADVENTURES OF THE FIRST WOMAN MOUNTIE

www.laurieschramm.ca

Laurie Schramm